AUSTIN

JONES

and the

Bracers of

Justice

Written

by

Quintan Bizzell

Printed in the United States of America.

Edited by Dale Kinkaid

Cover design by Dale Kinkaid

ISBN - Paperback: 979-8-218-72791-8

Quintan Bizzell

I dedicate this book to my children, and all of the children in my family.

Make time for your imagination and creativity.

Contents

A Quest for a Hero Begins

Planet Murn, just outside the Milky Way galaxy, was once cloaked in secrecy by a strange device called the Harmonic Defense System (aka the HDS). This unique device makes the planet invisible to negative energy, making it a completely and utterly peaceful planet full of love and happiness.

However, on August 6, 1945, in Earth's measurement of time, the Harmonic Defense System suffered damage and failed, causing the planet to be seen. A tremendous explosion shook the entire galaxy and beyond, causing massive damage to the once-great HDS. After the defense system went down, the dark days began.

From 1945 to the present day, the planet slowly started to change. Plants began to wilt, animals started to attack each other and the beings they once lived together with in harmony.

The darkness began to spread to the more advanced inhabitants of the planet.

First with greed, then theft, and eventually murder.

After the first murder was committed, it became a ritual for the elders to gather together and pray in front of the HDS in hopes that it would start working again.

The HDS was designed by the Ancient Elders using ancient technology. No one on the planet today knows or understands how to fix the machine.

Planet Murn is inhabited by a species thought to be half tropical cat, half human-like peaceful beings that pray to the Elders of the light. They are said to walk on their hind legs and can understand and speak any language that is spoken to them almost instantly. They call themselves the Wachooti, and they possess several psychic abilities. One well-known ability is to cloak themselves from other beings while only being able to be seen by other Wachooti, unless they are terrified. The species has also been known to hypnotize other low-willpower creatures to manipulate them to do their bidding.

None of the Wachooti people are over 5 feet tall except Dineckdin. The Wachooti people make fun of him due to his size and the amount of food he consumes.

Long ago, it was said that any Wachooti over 5 feet tall was linked to the ancient bloodline that started life on Planet Murn.

Dineckdin was considered a weirdo or black sheep due to his appearance and differing views from the other Wachooti people. His views on life, science, and religion always appeared to go against the grain. For instance, he did not believe in worshipping a machine that generated light like the rest of the Wachooti people. He always thought that there was more.

In school, he excelled in science and technology. He thought of himself as a great inventor and innovator. In comparison, everyone else wanted to be kings, queens, or rulers of the Wachooti.

None of the Wachooti had a vision of science or technology, so he was frowned upon when he came to his elders or parents with his inventions. Dineckdin always knew that one day, they would all praise him for his inventions, and he would gain the respect of the elders. This was the only vision that kept him determined to make the next great gadget.

Instead of worshipping the HDS, he spent most of his days studying how it worked. Planet Murn is a small planet with a tropical climate. Its environment is very moist and lush, filled with many different types of fruit trees, rivers, and lakes. The entire planet is in harmony, and upon any disturbance, every life form, from insects to the Wachooti people, can feel that something is wrong.

It is said that a select few of the elders can channel the first animal or insect to feel the disturbance and see through the eyes of the animal to detect the source of the disturbance. The Wachooti people are very sensitive, almost psychic. Some say this is due to the abundance of a mineral called Wachootium.

Wachootium is a unique type of quartz crystal with powers that include the sacred energy of piezoelectricity. No one on the planet knows how to harness the power of Wachootium.

Only the ancients knew the secret of the precious crystal, but Dineckdin was sure that Wachootium was the power behind the HDS.

While exploring one day, he began daydreaming about a pair of old leather bracers he found in an abandoned Wachootium mine. He found a way to combine Wachootium and the bracers. They helped him double, sometimes triple, his lifting power when helping the elders move large items or other daily activities. The Wachooti elders thought he possessed great strength since he was the biggest Wachooti. Still, he knew that the power of Wachootium combined with his mind produced a type of super strength.

The strange thing about the connection between the mind and Wachootium is that if he didn't think he could lift giant stones, the Wachootium would not work.

He had been studying this connection for quite some time. After secretly adding more and more Wachootium to the bracers, testing his strength, and being successful on so many occasions, he found a secret use for Wachootium that none of the others could have ever imagined.

He couldn't figure out how the ancient Wachooti used it to power the HDS.

He observed and studied the artifact at least once or twice a week.

He would make drawings and fantasize about being the hero after repairing the artifact and restoring peace to his people.

While admiring the Wachootium within the HDS, he heard a scream from the sky and counted three large objects that looked like fireballs roaring toward the city.

Dineckdin began running to his lab as quickly as possible because he felt the worst was about to happen.

The screams from the three objects were so loud that animals could be seen stampeding in many groups everywhere. While running as fast as his short legs could go, he noticed an entire group of elders moving toward the HDS with smiles, chanting: "The time has finally come!"

They were excited to welcome the ancient Wachooti back to the planet at its most desperate time.

Dineckdin slowed down as he considered what they were chanting. The Wachooti people started coming out of every home and shop with smiles. Some grabbed their children and most prized possessions to present to the ancient Wachooti masters, who were about to bring peace and happiness back to the planet. Indeed, to them, it was a time to celebrate.

Dineckdin immediately began thinking of all the great inventions he could present to the only people who would understand his greatness.

"Oh yeah!" especially when they see he has figured out how to work with the ancient resource Wachootium. "FINALLY, I WILL BE RECOGNIZED!" he screamed.

He started running faster again. He ran so fast that he ran past his mother and father, who had stepped outside to see what the fuss was about. He quickly stopped, creating a dust cloud, and shouted.

"They're here!"

"Who's here?" they asked.

"The ancient ones!" he screamed.

"I'm going to show them my creations!"

Then he began running so fast that he tripped and slid face-first into a fallen tree, knocking himself out at the edge of town with no one in sight.

The objects in the sky were visible at this time as they slowly descended, and they were ships!

Giant ships are something that the Wachooti had never seen before, at least not this size.

In the junkyard on the planet, where most Wachooti are warned not to wander, there are old capsule-sized ships thought not to work. No one has ever taken the time to figure out how to operate or fix them. Dineckdin spent most of his childhood fantasizing about flying around in the sky, and that's where his passion for technology started. He tinkered around until he eventually learned how to power on the propulsion system and figure out the controls.

He did all of this in secret because the elders frowned upon him for wandering and tinkering with things considered possessions of the ancients. It was said to be a curse to disturb the ancient artifacts.

This only made Dineckdin more interested. He learned how everything worked but knew that if he flew the ancient artifact, the elders would catch and punish him.

Hundreds of Wachooti now stare into the sky at the giant ships hovering and flashing a series of lights.

The Wachooti could not interpret the flashing lights.

Someone in the crowd yells, "With the size of those ships, I bet they've come to take us to the great paradise that they have created for us."

Suddenly, a roar of mumbles fell over the giant crowd, and you could hear people talking about all the imaginary stuff they could think up.

A few minutes later, people started running to their homes to pack, wanting to be the first aboard the ships to paradise. You could feel the excitement as everyone smiled and chattered about their plans once they reached paradise. Three young Wachooti children, arguing about window seats on the great ships, started to tussle and dropped an aluminum can onto the ground near the ditch where Dineckdin had fallen, waking him up. As he sat up and witnessed the children fighting, he screamed, "Stop!" They all stopped and looked at him.

One child said, "How can you sleep at a time like this? The ancestors have arrived to take us to paradise, and I'm getting a window seat!"

Then the children took off screaming, "No, I'm getting the window seat!" to each other.

Dineckdin looked puzzled for a second, then suddenly everything came rushing back about what he was on his way to do. With a big grin, he jumped up and continued towards his lab to get his most significant invention to show his ancestors. He had several options to show them, but there was one thing that he was the proudest of, and he knew that they would love to see the bracers.

"Yes", he thought.

"That's it! They're going to love the bracers!"

While Dineckdin was running toward his lab, the giant ships were 100 feet above the field full of people and descending quickly toward them.

The Wachooti people could feel the force from the ship's engines.

They held their children, baskets of gifts, food, clothing, and other things to share.

The landing gear unfolded, and ramps emerged from the ships. The three large ships lowered themselves to the ground in a triangle formation, with the biggest ship at the head of the triangle, its huge cargo door opening.

The people's eyes got wider and all of the talking stopped immediately.

Cho-Goon screams, "THE TROOPS ARE READY!!" to his master, Lord Kull.

Cho-Goon stands at 4'7" and is a cross between humans and warthogs. He has a huge snout, stands upright, and is very muscular.

Cho-Goon shouts, "This day will be remembered as the day we became rulers of the galaxy!"

Cho-Goon nods to a reptilian creature with a 5-foot tail. It's wearing a helmet, shoulder pads, and peculiar padding on its legs.

The creature's eyes lit up red, and it did an about-face movement and started running to a square-like speaker with two buttons. He pushed the red button and yelled out a blood-curdling scream as thousands of identical soldiers rushed out of the doors and down the ramps towards the Wachooti people.

Dineckdin was running up with his prized invention while the troops rushed down the ships' ramps.

The sounds of cheering immediately changed to screams of terror as the troops began grabbing people and putting collars around their necks. The collars were connected by chains that seemed to be electrified.

Dineckdin's eyes widened with terror, and he was in disbelief. He saw a massive creature, at least 10 feet tall! It was wearing a black suit with a clear visor over its eye that was lighting up with numbers and shapes. It rushed down the ramp, grabbed an innocent bystander by the neck, lifted him off of the ground over its head, and laughed. The bystander went limp and passed out. The creature cocked back and launched him at least 50ft into a crowd of terrified Wachooti as they began running towards the village.

Dineckdin freaked out, gathered his invention, and started running. He thought he had never seen anything that big and strong while living with the Wachooti.

His mind was racing,

"My parents, what do I do?"

He thought, "I need to get help." He said, "I need to get to the spaceship and find a hero."

He made it to the ship with tears in his eyes; he powered on the ship; he could hear the screams and see buildings on fire as he rose above his home.

The only area he could think of going towards was the place that generated the powerful explosion that damaged the harmonic defense system all of those years ago.

He thought, "I need to find someone capable of that kind of power to save my planet. Earth. Earth is where I will find a hero." He set the coordinates and flew off.

Waukegan, Illinois, USA, Earth 2017

A small city just outside of the big city of Chicago, this area is just off of Lake Michigan. There is a good mix of black, Hispanic, and Caucasian Americans. Just below the poverty line, you find gangs, drugs, and a high crime rate, just like any other highly populated city on Earth. Who knew this would be where the stage would be set for the greatest battle of good versus evil?

Random guy: "Jimmy, Jimmy! I heard about the fight that you won last month brotha! I also heard that you made a killing betting on yourself!"

Jimmy (with a grin): "Hey, hey, that's rumors man! Where are you getting your info from?"

They both laugh and as the older gentleman passes, Jimmy says: "Take one of these and tell everybody to come out and support the south side." The older of the two takes the flier with a picture of Jimmy on it, hands raised, and a date for his next boxing match. The old man skims the flyer up and down with a grin, "Yeah, the south side!"

Jimmy is a neighborhood boxing superstar. Boxing has been his passion since he was six when he got his first pair of gloves as a Christmas gift. He's 25 now and has quickly risen to the top of the amateur boxing scene. He expects that any day now, he'll be making millions with the title "World's Greatest Boxer."

He was a happy, upbeat guy that all the kids wanted to be like. He was a ladies' man who always kept his appearance up, spoke with respect, and even helped old ladies carry their groceries. This guy was perfect.

Who wouldn't want to be like him? Always into something athletic as a kid, Jimmy would excel to become the best. With a boxing record of 22-0, he has his name in the rafters for being one of the greatest on the southside, but he wanted more. Jimmy and some of his loyal followers were almost out of flyers, so they headed to the car. They heard bass booming so loud that you had to stop whatever you were doing to look.

Simultaneously, Jimmy's friends Alex and Rico say: "Here he comes!"

They referred to Jimmy's older brother, "OC".

OC is a nightmare to Jimmy's friends because he always pushes them around and regularly embarrasses them.

As the car slowly comes to a stop, OC says: "What up, Lil bro?" Jimmy, annoyed by the sight of his brother, answers: "Nothing much, just leaving."

OC: "Aren't you supposed to be training?"

Jimmy: "Aren't you supposed to be leaving?"

OC: "Yeah, anyways, I got a job for you."

OC reaches over to the passenger side and grabs a backpack, then hops out of the vehicle and shoves the backpack into Jimmy's chest.

With an angry stare into Jimmy's eyes, he says: "Drop this off to Dad, and DON'T be late this time."

Jimmy asks: "Why can't you do it?"

OC says abruptly: "Because I told YOU to do it! And last time I had to explain why you were late, so like I said, DON'T BE LATE THIS TIME."

At that moment, Rico steps forward and says: "We won't be late this ti–"

Before he could get the word out, OC palms Rico's face and, pushes him towards the car, stares at Alex angrily, and says: "I wasn't talking to you bums; I was talking to my brother!"

Then Jimmy says: "I have stuff to do!"

"Is it more important than this?" OC answers, "OK, then you can tell Dad why you can't do it."

Jimmy answers: "Fine."

OC lets out a slight chuckle as he gets back into his car, turns the volume up loud, and slowly creeps off down the street.

Aggravated, Jimmy says: "Let's go." And hops into the car as Rico asks: "Why is he always so mad?"

Jimmy answers: "I have been trying to figure that out all my life." As the three drive off, Jimmy says: "I'm going to drop you guys off; I have to go see my dad."

OC was known around town as a gangster, cold-blooded when it came to getting money. He is also the muscle in Jimmy's father's organization, which means if someone owes and can't pay, OC was sent to persuade you, and you didn't want that. People around town who grew up with OC often whispered that "OC" stood for "Outta Control" because of his history of anger issues and being an extreme bully during High School. From serving time in juvenile detention centers to spending years in and out of prison, he earned the label of a career criminal.

OC loved only three things: his father, Jimmy, and, most of all, money! If anything, or anyone, came between those things, he would make it his mission to destroy it.

OC always admired how Jimmy grew up to be a good kid. He loved that Jimmy never lost his cool or resorted to violence as he did.

At the same time, he grew jealous of Jimmy's small-town fame and often called him soft, labeling him a pretty boy who never got his hands dirty.

No matter what he or anyone else had to say about Jimmy, one thing was for sure: Everyone knew that he was the greatest boxer they had ever witnessed.

After dropping Alex and Rico off, Jimmy headed to his father's home to drop off the backpack.

Upon arrival, his father sat inside his garage with the door open at a card table with his long-time friend and bodyguard "Mack."

As Jimmy walks up, Mack says: "And the new champion of the world!"

Jimmy laughs and says: "What's up, big Mack?"

Mack says: "You ready for your next fight, champ?"

Jimmy says: "You already know Big Mack."

Mack says: "That's good, I can't wait!"

When the two finish catching up, Jim asks Mack to give him and Jimmy some privacy to chat.

As the door closes, Jim asks Jimmy: "How are you doing?'

Jimmy: "I'm doing all right, I guess."

Jim: "I'm worried about your brother."

Jimmy: "What did he do now?"

Jim: "I think he's getting mixed up with some hardheads from the west side. He's been spending a lot of time over there, and I don't like it."

Jimmy: "OK, Dad, I'll keep an eye on him. Speaking of OC, he told me to drop this off to you."

He hands his father the backpack and sits back down. His father opens the bag filled with hundred-dollar bills wrapped in rubber bands, grabs two stacks, and hands the money to Jimmy. He says: "Alright, I need to get myself some supper; you hungry?"

Jimmy says: "No thanks, I need to get to the gym and tighten up.

Jimmy's father is a well-known, respected man on the south side. He was viewed as a mob boss or a "made man." A very straightforward, fair, and humble individual who had a rough life growing up. He was always seen giving money to the kids in the neighborhood, and when there were issues between rival gang members, he was the one who brought everyone together, ending the feud. He was a true "OG" to the whole South Side, and they loved him.

Jimmy jumped into his car and cranked the ignition. While the car was running, a large grin stretched across his face because he remembered the big wad of cash his father had given him for delivering the bag.

He thought: "Let me call Alex and Rico. We will go to the strip club and have a good time, and I can train tomorrow."

It had been almost 72 hours since Dineckdin left Planet Murn for the Planet Earth to find a hero.

The display had many flashing red lights inside the ship, which he had never flown any considerable distance in. He could sense that the ship wouldn't hold up for too long.

He knew he was hours, if not minutes, from making it to the planet of heroes to start his quest. He could see the Earth getting bigger and bigger as he got closer.

His imagination was running wild with expectations of what he would see. Since all he knew were stories of the great power and destruction that came from this planet, it was hard to envision what a species would look like from such a place. One thing is for sure: he knew they would be a giant super-strong species, and all he needed was one to help him save his planet. He also worried about being taken prisoner by such beings, being tortured, and never being able to go back and free his people.

"Will the bracers protect me from these powerful creatures?!?!" He thought.

He shook that thought off instantly and looked back as he entered the upper atmosphere of the giant blue planet "Earth."

As Jimmy slowly pulls up to Alex's house, he can see Alex outside, walking down from his porch to the street.

Alex and Rico were long-time friends; many believed they were brothers because of their similar looks. They both stood around 5'8", they were Puerto Rican and were pretty much inseparable, they basically talked the same. They even lived across the street from each other.

As Alex approached the car, Jimmy said: "Where's Rico?"

Alex says: "I told him that you were on the way!"

Rico walks up with a bowl of food, stuffing his face, and trying to put on his jacket after sitting the bowl on Jimmy's car.

Jimmy yells: "Man get that shit off my ride, man!"

Rico laughs and says: " Your car is a rust bucket."

Jimmy says: "Whatever, bum, get in! Yall ready to get faded tonight?"

Alex says: "Man, I'm broke as hell, but I got this", as he pulls out a rolled cigar filled with weed.

Jimmy says: "Don't worry bro, tonight it's on me" as he pulls out the stack of cash.

Alex and Rico yell out: "Aw shit!" as Jimmy hits the gas.

While driving, Jimmy says: "Where ya'll wanna go?"

Alex says: "We should go to that one spot that we hit last wee-" With a mouthful of food, Rico says: "We need to hit Stretch's tonight, yo!"

Jimmy and Alex both agree while Alex lights up the weed and they continue across town for a night out.

Sitting low in his car, OC was parked, waiting for Big Q to come out and discuss future business plans. You could hear the bass rumble, but the volume was down low as the exhaust pipe dripped. The shine from the giant chrome rims instantly made you feel like whoever the driver was must be a big deal!

Big Q is known as a smooth yet calculating gangster with a lot of clout from the west side. He and OC have had problems off and on about certain areas where the two gangs bumped heads over who controls what street, but because they grew up around each other and were cool, they never got into any scuffles.

Besides, Big Jim always calmed down every situation so that both sides could coexist without violence.

Big Q appears from between two houses, blowing smoke from his mouth. As he and three other individuals get closer to the car, Q hands what he was smoking to one of the others and tells them to chill for a minute.

OC and Q were meeting up to discuss a large shipment of drugs; both gangs were going to split up and potentially make millions.

The two have been secretly hanging out off and on for months now, planning their getaway from the streets. They were both ready to settle down with families, maybe even children.

As Big Q gets into the car, he says: "What up, OC?"

OC cracks a smile and says: "You already know Q, how's business?"

Q says: "Business is business; it could be better."

OC answers: "Ain't that the truth!" They both laugh.

OC asks: "So you sure everything is tight on your end? We don't need any surprises or hiccups when we make this move".

Big Q answers: "For the third time, man, everything is air-tight. You just need to make sure that you hold everything down on your end. The shipment is already on the boat and headed our way. You got the location locked down?"

OC answers: "No doubt"

Big Q says: "Cool, I have the truck; all we need to do is handle the exchange and split the product. After that, I'll see you somewhere on the beach in Hawaii!"

They both laugh and shake hands; Big Q exits the vehicle and slowly walks away with his crew back between the houses.

As he disappears, OC lifts his phone to go through his contacts to make sure that he has all of his personnel ready for what's to come.

As the music plays loud, Alex yells: "Hey yo, Jimmy!"

Jimmy answers: "Yoooo!"

Alex: "The dance floor is packed tonight!"

Jimmy: "I know, you see that honey over there?"

Alex: "Yeah, man, she is stacked!"

Jimmy: "She keeps looking my way, Ima go talk to her."

Rico: "Jimmy, I heard she is with Marshawn."

Jimmy: "Marshawn who?"

Alex: "Marshawn from the east side! Yeah, that's his girl."

Jimmy: "Well, not tonight!"

Rico: "Here we GO!"

Jimmy was known by his closest friends for becoming uncontrollable when under the influence of alcohol, especially when women were around. There were even times when he had given them black eyes for trying to calm him down during an alcohol-fueled rage. Most of the time, Jimmy is cool and calm, but when the alcohol kicks in, he changes into a different person, and that person is angry.

As Jimmy approaches the woman to talk, Alex and Rico move closer to each other so that they could converse.

Rico: "I got a feeling this won't end well."

Alex: "It never does."

Rico: "Why did we even come here?"

Alex: "It was your idea! Let's just hope for the best and stay posi-"

Just as Alex was talking, Marshawn walked into the bar smiling, admiring how lively the atmosphere was. He was ready to party.

Jimmy to the woman: "Hi."

The woman: "Hi."

Jimmy: "My name is-"

The woman interrupts with a smile: "I know who you are, you're Jimmy, right? King of the Southside? Don't you have a game coming up?"

Jimmy: "You mean a match, right? I'm a boxer. I saw you from across the room and had to come to find out what your name was."

She let out a slight giggle and said: "My name is Marcella."

Jimmy smiled: "That's a beautiful name."

As the two continued to talk, Rico and Alex came over to try to warn Jimmy about Marshawn.

Alex: "Heeey Jimmy, excuse me, sweetheart."

He scooted between the two.

"Jimmy, we should head out before it gets too late (he winked his eye and pointed towards Marshawn)."

Rico: "Yeah, it's getting a little too crowded in here." he also winks his eye.

Jimmy says: "You guys are acting weird, and we just got here. Now, if you will excuse me, Marcella and I were having a nice conversation before you two interrupted us, ain't that right Marcella?" Jimmy softly moves the two friends from between them.

Alex says: "Well, we tried," as he and Rico walked away.

While going back to their table, they could see Marshawn make a beeline towards Jimmy and Marcella.

He no longer looked like he was enjoying himself. He was followed by three other big guys.

You could feel the room's energy shift as they got closer to Jimmy.

Marcella says: "So Jimmy, you must be pretty nervous about your upcoming fight. I would be scared to fight someone with all those people watching!"

Jimmy: "Well, as a boxer, you train for the fight and not the crowd; you have to learn to block everything out. It takes time! Maybe I could show you around the gym sometime, and I can teach you a few things."

Just as he finishes his sentence, Marshawn arrives and says: "Oh really, you wanna take my girl and show her a few things?!"

You could hear his fist ball up like someone was squeezing a balloon. Jimmy heard it too but played it cool.

By this time, you could tell that something was going on, and all of the people who were talking got quiet and started paying attention to the conversation.

Out of the whispers, you heard someone say: "Hey, that's Jimmy."

Amid the stillness, Jimmy breaks the silence and says: "Yeah, women can learn how to box too! Maybe if you paid more attention to your lady instead of your boyfriends, you would be able to teach her a few things!"

Marshawn says: "Motherf –" and swings with his right hand with everything that he had.

Jimmy knew it was coming and effortlessly moved his head and neck backward, watching the punch go by in slow motion. As he quickly moved out of the way of the punch, Marshawn fell over from the force of his swing, knocking over drinks and a few chairs.

Jimmy moved swiftly to the closest of Marshawn's friends, grabbed him with both hands, and whirled him full speed into a table of three people, knocking them and the table over. He then turned to Marshawn (who had just recovered from the miss) and hit him full power with an overhand right with such force that it knocked his tooth out of his mouth, an instant knockout!

A third guy approached to take a shot while Jimmy wasn't looking, and out of nowhere, Alex smashes a wooden chair over his head, knocking him down.

Jimmy is now standing face-to-face with the last guy. The guy doesn't budge, as if he's frozen stiff; you can see him trembling.

Rico: "Hey! They called the cops! We gotta go… NOW!"

Alex approaches Jimmy and says: "Jimmy, Jimmy, YO!"

As if he snaps out of a trance, Jimmy shakes it off and says: "Ok, yeah, right, let's go."

He stares at the last guy on his way out of the door, ensuring he doesn't make a move.

Once outside, Rico says: "I told you she had a man. Now we got beef with cats from the Eastside man. Take me home!"

Jimmy: "Chill man, he swung on me first. Don't worry about those dudes on the East."

Rico: "You're an undefeated boxer; I'm a regular guy! Don't you get it?!?!"

Meanwhile, inside the club, a random guy finishes his drink and finds a tooth at the bottom of his glass.

Jimmy's phone lights up as he mutters: "Oh boy!"

Alex: "What now?"

Jimmy: "My brother needs me to meet him; I gotta drop you guys off and make a play."

Rico: "BET"

Alex: "You sure you don't need me to roll?"

Jimmy: "Nah, I gotta do this solo... I think I hurt my hand," as he laughs.

Alex joins in the laughter: "That shit was crazy!" as they drive back towards the southside.

Half asleep, Dineckdin hears a pop and feels a slight rumble as he notices fire around the ship. He starts to panic; in that same instance, all the lights inside begin blinking. His first thought was that he would fail and that this was where he would die, never returning to save his planet. The ship started to move faster toward the Earth, and a great rumbling began to shake the ship uncontrollably. After about 10 minutes, the rumbling stopped, and all the electronics had failed leaving Dineckdin in complete darkness speeding into the planet's atmosphere.

He screamed: "Oh powerful great elders, I know you did not bring me this far to leave me to die!"

He stared out the window, seeing lights and structures whizzing by.

He thought to himself: "Well, this is it."

Air Traffic Control: "Radio one, can you switch to the private channel?"

Three men in the traffic control tower watched an unknown object moving at incredible speeds across their radar.

Air Traffic Control #2, on the private channel: "Roger Control 1, go ahead."

Air Traffic Control #1: "Do you see what we see over southeastern Illinois?"

Air Traffic Control #2: "Wow, what do you think that is?"

Air Traffic Control #1: "No clue, but we will try-"

A man in a car with his wife and three kids: "I'm not too familiar with taking this way to the high- WOW, that airplane is way too close- WAIT, it's gone!!"

As lights appeared over the car, they disappeared just as quickly.

The wife asks: "What?"

Man: "I just saw a UFO over the car."

Wife: "Really?!? Are you sure?"

Man: "I thought it was a plane flying low, and then it just vanished!"

The little boy in the back seat: "Dad, are you smoking crack?"

While Dineckdin shed tears as if he'd given up, all of the systems came back online, and he pulled up on the steering control as hard as he could.

As the ship leveled out, he screamed: "Thank the elders, we did it!"

He reduces his speed and takes in all the structures and views of this strange new world he has just entered. It's a few hours after sundown, so everything is dark, and there's not much to see, but he's still fascinated and excited about what's to come. He notices that there is a lot of water and recognizes it because there is water on Planet Murn.

A spark of electricity arcs up close to his left hand, and the power goes out again.

Dineckdin yells: "Not again!"

The craft drops on a vertical path straight down at least 1000ft and splashes into Lake Michigan, sizzling and bubbling as it sinks deep into the lake bed.

In the darkness, Dineckdin fumbles around to find the issue and tries to repair it, but he cannot see.

Whatever went wrong with the ship was likely an easy fix, is what Dineckdin was thinking.

He checked to see if any water was getting into the ship as it sank to the floor of the lake.

While feeling around in the dark, the power returned, and the ship accelerated, slamming him against the ship's wall.

The ship's movement through the water at such high speed caused an 11-foot wave of water. A couple walking along the lakefront spotted this wave and watched in amazement as the water sprayed into the air like a water spout.

Dineckdin grabbed the device that controlled the acceleration and shut it down.

The malfunctioning ship was a problem, but Dineckdin thought, "There are bigger issues at hand that need to be dealt with, and finding a hero is the top priority."

"Ahh, yes! Time to do what I have set out to do."

He ran to the back of the ship and grabbed the bracers.

With the ship underwater, Dineckdin felt safe abandoning it where it was. Water rushed in as he opened the door, pushing him to the floor again. He put the bracers into his mouth and swam to the surface.

OC: "Jimmy!"

Jimmy walks into the warehouse and says: "Chill, OC! I got here as soon as I could, man. What are you all worked up about?"

OC: "Look, man, I need you to help me out tonight, and nobody needs to know about it, especially not Dad!"

Jimmy: "He's already sniffing something!"

OC: "What do you mean?"

Jimmy: "He knows you've been hanging out with someone on the west side, and he doesn't like it. He thinks you're up to something."

OC: "Well, we can't worry about that now."

Jimmy: "Wait, what do you mean WE?"

OC: "Look, I just need you to ride with me to make this deal and keep your mouth shut, OK?!?!"

Jimmy: "Oh wow! So now you're making deals behind Dad's back?!?!"

OC: "Man, look, I don't want to work for Dad for the rest of my life, and this is my first step towards being my own boss. I don't need any hiccups, Jimmy! This shit needs to go smooth. Just this one time, and I swear you will never have to worry about me bugging you again. As a matter of fact, I won't be bothering any of you for anything else."

Jimmy: "Somehow, I doubt it, but okay, OC. This is it, and if you get into a jam, do not tell Dad that I was with you like you did that one time, okay?!?"

OC: "BET! Ok, here's the plan. Me and you are gonna roll up to the docks separately. I'll get there first and go in. You are in charge of the fellas holding down the outside, got it?!"

Jimmy: "Got it."

OC, taking a few sniffs: "ARE YOU DRUNK?"

Jimmy: "I had a few drinks, but I'm not dr-"

OC: "Get a coffee and straighten up; it's almost showtime."

As Dineckdin swam to shore, he noticed several buildings nearby and decided to sneak over to one of them. While looking around outside the building, he saw lots of lights coming closer to the location where he was scouting, so he decided to hide.

OC and several others showed up at the dock warehouse just as planned. Shortly after Jimmy pulled up, he needed to use the restroom and knew he needed to make it quick so as not to disrupt anything. He snuck around to the back of the warehouse to pee.

Dineckdin notices a being moving in his direction from the lights that just pulled up.

He thought: "This is it, this is my chance."

Jimmy stood still in the front of the bushes, and Dineckdin got into position about 8 feet behind him.

The Wachooti species can cloak themselves to any species but their own, unless terrified, and Dineckdin wasn't sure of the reaction he would get when revealing himself to this new species.

Jimmy lets out a sigh of relief as he turns around to get back to his position up front.

Just as he turns around, he sees what he thinks to be a huge cat standing on its hind legs holding a pair of what looks to be gloves. The two both freeze in fear, looking each other up and down.

Jimmy: "What the hell?!?!"

Dineckdin: "What the hell?"

Jimmy: "Wait, you can talk?!"

Dineckdin: "Wait, you can talk?!"

Jimmy didn't know that Dineckdin was mimicking human language to learn to understand and speak it—another great skill of the Wachooti species.

Jimmy thought: "This can't be real right now. How can this cat talk?"

Dineckdin took three steps forward, and Jimmy moved back as soon as the cat-like creature made a move.

Dineckdin dropped the bracers on the ground and took a few steps back and, without his mouth moving, said: "Try these on." his eyes glowed an electric green.

Hearing the voice in his head, Jimmy says: "How'd you do that, and your EYES!!"

He felt an overwhelming urge to put the bracers on, almost as if he was hypnotized.

The bracers were on his hands; they tightened up and immediately disappeared.

Just as he looked up, his phone rang.

Startled by the phone ringing, Dineckdin cloaked himself and hid.

Jimmy answered the phone.

OC: "Jimmy, where are you, man? I told you that I don't need any hiccups!"

Jimmy: "I stepped out back to take a leak. I'm on my way back to position, man. Chill!"

OC: "Good, hurry up! The truck will be here shortly!"

Dineckdin noticed lots of movement around the building where he met his newfound hero. He secretly followed the hero to a few ships. These ships were odd because they did not fly—they rolled!

He found a good hiding spot to watch. It looked like the hero and several other beings were waiting for something to happen, and Dineckdin wanted a front seat.

OC sent Jimmy a text that said: "Look alive. He's about to pull up."

Jimmy tells the other guys: "Heads up, it's showtime."

In the distance, you could hear a vehicle approaching the warehouse area. Dineckdin spotted two lights coming close and going into the structure where all the action was. As the truck pulled up, to his surprise, Jimmy noticed that the passenger was Big Q from the west side. He did not recognize the driver, and the truck was being followed by four more cars.

Jimmy texts OC: "You sure you don't need me inside for backup?"

OC replies: "Nah, I don't need you here to mess things up. I got it!"

As the truck pulled into the warehouse, the doors closed, leaving the four cars and personnel outside with Big Q, OC, and the delivery man inside the warehouse.

Big Q and the delivery guy (Angelo) get out of the truck.

Big Q says: "Hold on, OC. Let me show this man to his ride," as he walks Angelo outside. From outside the warehouse, Jimmy sees the door crack open, and Big Q and the truck driver walk to the car closest to the road. Big Q opens the passenger door for Angelo to get in. Once he's in, the vehicle starts up, and Big Q goes back inside and shuts the warehouse door.

Big Q: "Alright, let's get down to business!"

OC: "Hell yeah, man, I'm ready!"

Big Q opens the back of the truck, and they both stand there amazed by how many bricks are stacked up.

OC: "Man, this is it!" with a smile.

Big Q: "I brought something to celebrate." He goes to the truck's passenger side and pulls out an alcoholic beverage and two Styrofoam cups. At the back of the truck, he places the cups on the bumper, pours the drinks, and hands one to OC. Here's to retirement!"

OC: "To retirement and frozen umbrella drinks on the beach!" they laugh and guzzle down their drinks.

OC: "Let's get moving."

Big Q puts the bricks into OCs trunk one by one until he gets to the sixth brick.

He calls to OC: "Ay man, look at the symbol on this one in the back!"

OC rushes over to look. He ducks his head halfway into the trunk and takes a look.

He says: "What's the problem? I don't see any-"

At that moment, Big Q pulls out a pistol and hits OC on the back of his head, knocking him out.

Quickly looking around to make sure no one noticed, he grabbed OC and dumped him into the trunk with the drugs, and closed it.

He then called 911 and disguised his voice.

Big Q: "Hello"

911 Operator: "911, what is your emergency?"

Big Q: "Hello, I'd like to report some suspicious activity at Dock 8. Lots of guys with guns, and I think they are hurting people!!"

He hangs up the phone and jumps into the truck. He blows the horn twice to signal the door to be opened, and the truck starts rolling out of the building.

Noticing all of the movement, Jimmy thought: "Good, must be time to go."

Jimmy tells the guys it's time to wrap things up as he walks toward the building entryway.

Big Q slows down and says: "Tell ya brother, I said thanks for all the help!" and laughs as he drives off.

The way that he said what he said didn't sit well with Jimmy, so he rushed into the building to see that his brother was nowhere to be found.

He immediately called OC and heard his phone ringing from the trunk. Fearing the worst, he tried to open the trunk, but it was locked.

He ran outside and saw Big Q pointing his way and telling his goons to get Jimmy as he sped off onto the street.

Two men start running towards Jimmy, and the other three rush to get into the cars they came in.

Angrily, Jimmy clenches his fists and bites down, takes one step with his left foot, leans back, and delivers a powerful punch with his right hand to the chest of the first man to approach, sending him flying backward into the next approaching man, knocking both of them down.

The man who absorbed the punishing punch immediately held his chest and arched his back in pain, flopping around like a fish out of water.

Dineckdin's eyes widened with amazement while watching his newfound hero in action. When the other men in the car saw what had happened, they drove off. Jimmy ran up to the back of the car just in time. He slammed both fists on the trunk, screaming: "Where's my brother?!?!?" He hit the trunk so hard that the car slightly popped a wheelie, causing sparks to fly from underneath.

The driver hits the gas pedal and speeds off, leaving Jimmy crying in the middle of the street in front of the warehouse. He ran to his car just in time to hear sirens. He starts the car and yells for the crew to run because the police are coming.

As the swat team raids the warehouse, they find it empty, except for one car. As they approach the car, they hear a ringing from the trunk. The officer in charge grabs the key from the ignition. As he opens the trunk, OC opens his eyes to several police officers pointing guns and telling him to get out of the trunk. They removed the gun from his waist and the drugs from the trunk and hauled him off to jail.

Quintan Bizzell

Austin's Story

Beep beep beep!!

The sound of an alarm goes off in the hallway of a small apartment.

His eyes are half open, and he is not awake. He smells smoke and jumps up in a panic.

Running frantically down the hallway, he finds the living room on fire, with his mother asleep in an old recliner.

He screams: "Mom!!"

His mother mumbles a few words and turns to go back to sleep. The young boy rushes up, grabs his mother by the arm, and drags her from the chair towards the door.

Suddenly, she wakes up and starts panicking, screaming: "OH MY GOD!!"

They move to the hallway and down the stairs to go outside. The building was evacuated, and the fire department put out the fire in the small apartment.

The Fire Chief gathers everyone together to make an announcement.: "The source of the fire was a lit cigarette that ignited the carpet in apt #7b. Luckily, we contained and put the fire out, but nothing can be recovered from the blaze."

With tears in his eyes, the boy looks at his mother and says: "You fell asleep with a LIT CIGARETTE?!"

At the same time, the building's landlord and the fire chief approached the young boy's mother and asked: "Are you Bonnie?"

Bonnie replies: "Yes."

Landlord: "May I have a word with you?"

The three walk off to the back of a squad car, and you can tell they are having a heated discussion.

As Bonnie walks back to the boy, he can see tears in her eyes. He asks: "What happened?"

She answers: "We have to find another place to live," and starts sobbing uncontrollably.

The young boy, Austin Jones, and his mother, Bonnie, had just gotten acclimated to this new apartment after being evicted. This was already the second home they had to leave due to some unfortunate event. Austin is 15 years old now and barely remembers his father being a presence in his life. All he remembers is that his mother told him that his father took off with another woman to pursue his music career.

He and his mother have been alone, and his mother doesn't seem to be able to recover from the abandonment. The two begin to walk back up to the apartment to see the aftermath of the fire, mainly to see if there was anything that they could salvage. As they open the door, they can't believe their eyes. The living room and the kitchen were completely charred and unrecognizable. The hallway leading to the bedrooms was charred halfway, and the rest was covered in soot. To both of their surprise, though, the bedrooms were not damaged. They began collecting what wasn't burned to a crisp or soaking wet. It was now 6 am, and they could start to see the sunrise through the soot-stained windows of the apartment. The fire started late Saturday night; now it was Sunday morning, and Austin could only think about school on Monday.

Lots of kids from school lived in his building and rode the same bus, so he knew he would be the talk of the school on Monday, probably forever. While he and his mother were taking things to the trash, they left the apartment door slightly cracked. While inside the bedrooms cleaning up, Austin heard the scuffle of footsteps coming from the front door. He moved into the living room to see what the noise was.

The door was cracked, so he opened it slowly. A girl was standing there, eyes widening as she scanned the charred remains of the apartment. Austin had seen her before, on the bus and at school. He knew she was younger than he was because of her grade level. While he's remembering, she says: "DAAAAANNNG!! It looks like a bomb blew up in here!!"

Austin says: "I know, and now we have to move out."

He says: "I've seen you before; what's your name?"

She says: "I'm Brianna. I don't live in this building; I live a few blocks away, but I heard what happened here and came to take a look."

Austin says: "Hey, don't you ride my bus?"

Brianna says: "Yeah, I hate that ugly bus!"

Growing up, Austin never really had friends since he and his mother moved around so much, so he gave up on trying.

This time, though, it felt different. Brianna started helping Austin haul things to the dumpster, and they quickly became friends.

Jimmy's phone rings.

Jimmy: "DAD!!"

Jim: "What's going on, Jimmy?"

Jimmy: "OCs in trouble!"

Jim: "I heard."

Jimmy: "Wait, how do you know?"

Jim: "The real question is, how do you know, Jimmy?! Get over here. I have something I want you to see."

Jimmy: "Ok," and he hangs up the phone. Jimmy says to himself: "DAMN! I'm DEAD."

As Dineckdin watches his new hero, he recognizes that something is wrong, but he continues to watch and follow him to see what great things he will do.

Since their encounter, he hasn't had the courage to ask the new hero to help save his planet, but the urgency is definitely building.

He now sits in Jimmy's back seat, completely cloaked, less than 5 feet away, wondering what's next.

Jimmy is panicking at this point. First, he meets a creature that gives him a pair of gloves.

Next, his brother gets kidnapped. Now, his father is going to kill him because it's all his fault for not telling him what was going on in the first place.

He's freaking out as he pulls up to his father's house.

Exiting the car, he notices more cars than usual, as if his father has company.

"What is going on?!?" he thinks to himself.

Jimmy walks up to the door, and right before he knocks, it opens.

Mack says: "Jimmy, what the hell is going on? Your father is out for blood."

As the three (Dineckdin was close behind monitoring Jimmy's every move) walked down into the basement, Jimmy noticed plastic hanging from the ceiling to the floor.

When he got closer, he noticed that plastic was also lining the floor.

Mack pulled an opening in the plastic back and gestured for Jimmy to enter. Inside stood a couple of Jim's most loyal henchmen and two guys tied to a pole.

Jimmy's father was frantically pacing back and forth, and it was clear that he was upset.

Dineckdin could feel the anger and tension, but it was too late for him to run away, so he found a corner and kept watching.

Jim: "Finally, now we can get some answers!"

Jimmy: "Ok, Dad, you might not believe me but -

Jim: "Take the bags off of them!"

The two henchmen walk over and remove the bags, covering their faces.

Jimmy screams: "Those are the guys who took OC!"

The two guys see Jimmy, and their eyes widen with fear as Jimmy approaches them. They both start squirming and trying to get loose.

Mack yells: "Now, now, Jimmy."

Jimmy ignores Mack and swings a right-handed punch at one of the guys. The guy just so happens to duck his head, causing Jimmy to punch the pole. The punch was so strong that it bent the pole and knocked screws out of the top, causing them to fall to the floor. Jimmy goes into a frenzy, beating both men with lefts and rights relentlessly while screaming: "WHERE IS MY BROTHER?!?!"

Then he hears Jim yell: "That's enough!"

Both men were left doubled over, bleeding from their noses and mouths.

Jim yells to the two men: "Where's my money?!" as he pulls out an aluminum bat.

Jimmy says: "Your son is missing, and all you can think about is money!?!"

Jim yells: "Your brother is in jail! I told you to watch him because I knew that he was up to something stupid (he stands up with the bat) with these no good (he swings and hits one guy with the bat) backstabbing (he hits the other guy in the arm with the bat) losers from the west side.

Jimmy says: "OC is in jail?!"

Jim: "Yes, and he's not getting out this time! He took about 500K from me; he was planning to take it and run off with his new buddies from the west side! (as he delivered another swing of the bat). They double-crossed him and set him up to take the fall. Now he's gone for good, and so is my money."

Jimmy stood there completely confused while replaying the last conversation that he and OC had before everything happened.

Dineckdin couldn't believe what he was seeing. His newfound hero was torturing beings that were tied up and could not fight back. He thought to himself: "This is not what being a hero is about, he had seen enough!"

Jim pulls the slide back on a large pistol and sets it on a table. "Now it's time for some answers!"

Mack says: "Jimmy, I think you should go home now," as he pulls the plastic back and gestures for him to walk out. He walks him upstairs to the door, and just before the door closes, the gun fires twice, causing Jimmy, Dineckdin, and Mack to all jump.

Bonnie: "Austin!"

Austin jumps up out of his sleep and realizes that his mother was calling his name, he hates when she does that.

Bonnie: "Time to get up and get ready for school."

Austin drags himself out of bed and begins to get ready. Then suddenly, there is a knock at the door.

Bonnie opens the door and Brianna comes in eyes closed.

Brianna: "You must be an early bird like me; my mom calls me the early bird. Hey, did your mom make anything for breakfast?"

Bonnie: "Um, I am his mom!"

Brianna, after opening her eyes and paying attention: "Oooh, my bad Mrs. Jones, Is Austin here?"

Bonnie: "Yes, he's getting ready now. Try your best to have a seat and excuse the house."

Bonnie walks to the back towards the bathroom and whispers to Austin: "That little girl is here for you" and winks her eye. Austin says: "Come on Mom" and spits toothpaste out of his mouth.

Austin was surprised to see Brianna waiting for him in the charbroiled kitchen.

She sees him come out and says: "About time. Are you ready?"

He says: "Not really," as the two walk out of the door and head to the bus stop.

Austin was quiet during the walk, and looking down at the ground. Brianna says: "Don't worry about it; today's gonna go smooth."

As the two approached the bus stop, they couldn't help but notice that everyone was staring, some giggling, but no one said anything. As they all got on the bus, everything seemed pretty normal. Austin couldn't help but think: "Maybe today WILL go smoothly."

Dineckdin opens his eyes to the sound of a ringing noise. It was morning by the looks of the sun through the window, and he realized that he had accidentally fallen asleep. He had gone home with Jimmy and watched him frantically pace back and forth all night, talking to himself about the entire situation until the early hours. Dineckdin fell asleep, waiting for the opportunity to steal the bracers back. All of the events that led up to this moment helped him to decide that this person was not the hero that would help to save his people, and now he needed to get the bracers and get back to the mission.

Jimmy sits up from his phone ringing and answers: "Hello?"

Rico: "What's up bro?! You good?"

Jimmy: "Yeah, I got a bad headache, and everything went wrong last night."

Rico: "Whaaaaat, you mean worse than what happened before you dropped us off?"

Jimmy: "Maan, way worse!"

Rico: "Get dressed, let's go get some grub."

Jimmy: "Cool, give me like 45 minutes."

Rico: "Ok, cool."

Just as Jimmy was going to get up and get into the shower, he thought: "What about those strange gloves that the cat thing gave me? I don't think I should get them wet. What WAS that cat thing?" As he thought about removing the bracers, they started to uncloak and loosen.

Jimmy said to himself: "This is crazy!"

He took the bracers off and left the room to take a shower.

Dineckdin's eyes widened at the sight of Jimmy taking the bracers off and leaving the room. He jumped down from the shelf, grabbed the bracers, and quickly moved toward the front door of the apartment. While quickly tip-toeing through the apartment, he spotted a large white door with two handles.

He thought to himself: "I wonder what's in there?"

He grabbed the handle that he could reach and pulled it, and an amazing bright light came on.

Dineckdin's eyes glowed with happiness and excitement, for he had found a treasure chest.

He immediately began grabbing meats and cheese and eating as if he had never eaten before. He didn't know what he was eating, but he knew that it was wonderful. He grabbed a vase-looking pitcher that had a bright red liquid inside of it. He took a sip from the vase, and his tastebuds went crazy! He held it out in front of him with two hands and stared at it for a few seconds; then, he drank it so fast that the liquid spilled from both sides of his mouth until the vase slipped from his hands, hit the floor, and shattered.

Jimmy heard the noise, peeked out of the shower, and asked: "Who's there?"

At that moment, Dineckdin ran and opened the front door, then took off running, leaving the door wide open.

The school bell rang.

The day was almost over, and Austin was shocked that the day had gone as well as it had. Nobody mentioned anything. As he walked through the hallway, he was tapped on the shoulder; it was Brianna: "See, I told you everything would be cool today."

Austin: "You were right, thanks!"

Brianna: "Hey, have you ever heard of a boxer named Jimmy from the Southside?"

Austin: "No, why?"

Brianna: "He's the best! I saw a flier that he's fighting soon. We should go check it out!"

Austin: "We have no money. How? Do you have some money I don't know about or something?"

Brianna: "Don't worry about that. I sneak in all the time through the back door early and wait for the fight. I'll show you later!"

The second bell rings.

"Gotta go!" said Brianna.

Austin smiles big as he walks away to his next class. He has finally found a true friend. He enters his social studies class, eager for the day to be over so that he can hang out with his new friend. His teacher, Mrs. Washington, announces to the class that they will be watching a movie about the Civil War today. As she starts the TV, it won't come on.

"Give me a minute; something is wrong."

A voice comes from the back of the classroom: "Does anyone smell smoke? Maybe it's on fire!" Austin turns around and notices all the kids in the class pointing, whispering, and giggling.

The voice was Deangelo, a known bully who rides Austin's bus. Austin turned back around, facing forward with embarrassment. He looked into the sky as he replayed how well the day was going, only to be set up and laughed at by everyone. As the giggles popped up from different directions behind him in class, Austin had no choice but to sit and take the punishment silently.

Mrs. Washington: "I've got it!"

The movie started to play, and Austin could instantly feel the energy shift. He was relieved. As the bell sounded, signaling the end of the school day, Austin couldn't wait to get home—most of all, to hang out with his new best friend, Brianna.

After meeting up with her in the hallway, the two head out to the bus line.

Brianna: "Hey, when we get off the bus, we should go down to Slumberland Gym so that I can show you how I sneak in.

Austin: "Are you sure we won't get into trouble?"

Brianna: "YES. Trust me, I'm a professional!"

Austin, laughing: "Yeah, right!!"

As they approach the bus, Austin gets on first, and he normally sits way in the back. While moving towards the back in a hurry, someone sticks their leg out, tripping him. He falls between two seats on top of his book bag. When he turns to see who had tripped him, he sees Deangelo and a few of his friends laughing.

Brianna rushed to help Austin and says: "Don't worry about it; he's just showing off for his cronies."

The two sit in the same seat at the back of the bus.

Brianna: "So, will you get in trouble if we walk to the gym as soon as we get off the bus? My mom doesn't care."

Austin: "I'm sure it'll be ok if we make it qui-"

Just before he could finish his last word, a big ball of paper hit him right in the face, followed by an eruption of laughter from all the kids on the bus. Austin stood up immediately and looked around. Just as he stood up, another piece hit him. Deangelo and two of his buddies slapped five and continued laughing.

Brianna: "Who was it?"

Austin: "Deangelo"

Brianna: "Again"

Brianna gets up, stares at Deangelo, and gets ready to move. Austin grabs her by the backpack and pulls her back into her seat.

Austin: "We don't need to get kicked off the bus."

Brianna: "I'm tired of him."

Austin: "Me too, but my mom will kill me if I get suspended from the bus; we don't have a car."

Brianna: "Ok, you're right, but I swear one of these days (she lowers her voice to a whisper) they'll get theirs."

The majority of the kids on the bus are from Austin's neighborhood. A large number of the students get off at the second-to-last stop. As the bus squeaks along, dropping the kids off, the two sit quietly in their seats, waiting patiently for their stop.

Dineckdin is now wandering around in the strange land again, alone. As he walks through the streets (cloaked), he sees heroes everywhere, just walking around. He even sees strange animals; he stops at the sight of a dog wandering by an alleyway. He snaps his fingers to get the animal's attention. As the dog turns around, Dineckdin uncloaks and stares into the dog's eyes. The swirly clockwise movements of Dineckdin's pupils catch the dog's attention. Dineckdin mentally tells the dog he wants a white treasure chest of food. He does this by showing the dog images. The dog goes back into the yard from where it had escaped, and Dineckdin follows. As he gets closer, he can hear a repeating thud over and over again. As he approaches the sound, he finds the dog running its head into the door over and over. He then goes over to the door and turns the knob. The door was unlocked, and it opened right up. The dog walked right to the kitchen and started running into the refrigerator over and over again.

Dineckdin saw the refrigerator and smiled so big. He quickly opened the door and began rifling through the food inside. Again, everything that he tasted was delicious, all that he could think about was how to get a treasure chest onto the ship to take home with him. As he enjoyed the food, the dog was still thumping his head against the side of the refrigerator, causing several boxes of cereal to shake towards the edge of the top of the fridge.

Dineckdin could hear someone laughing in the distance. The laugh was quiet, making him think of the small Wachooti children playing outside on his home planet of Murn. He began to feel sad as the visions of those same children being captured and locked up filled his thoughts. A cereal box finally falls from the top of the refrigerator, causing Dineckdin to snap out of what he was thinking and remember where he was. A baby hero stands there smiling and giggling as he closes the refrigerator. As the two stand face to face, the baby says: "Cat!" and laughs uncontrollably.

Dineckdin, not knowing what the word meant, starts laughing with the baby hero. He felt a genuine connection with the hero species for the first time since landing on the planet. Large heavy footsteps from above started getting closer. The uncontrollable laughter must have disturbed a larger, full-grown hero.

Dineckdin made a run for the door and ran back out to the street. A mother came into the kitchen to find her dog ramming his head against the refrigerator and her baby boy laughing uncontrollably. She picked up the baby as he says: "Cat, go bye-bye." As the mother carries the baby to the back door, she gives a quick glance outside and shuts the door. The dog returned to normal and looked confused at the back door as it shut.

Dineckdin has been cloaked walking the streets in fear and wonder while observing the huge vehicles and heroes everywhere. He is starting to feel hopeless on his mission to save his home. With so many options, how would he know which hero would be the right one? He climbs up to the top of a tree, sits down, and presses his hands to his face in frustration. A swarm of sad thoughts floods his mind of what could be happening to his family and the others on his planet being tortured. The replay of the screams of the victims as they were being attacked starts ringing loudly in his head, and angry tears start running down his face.

Brianna: "Maybe we can stop by Mr. Taos and get a free egg roll."

Austin: "What?!? We can get free eggrolls?"

Brianna: "Sometimes, if we pass out fliers"

As the bus pulls up for the majority of the kids to get off, you can hear the ruffling of backpacks as they are put on before the bus stops.

Since Austin and Brianna were at the back of the bus, naturally, they were the last to get off. As they stepped down from the bus, they both heard a voice quietly say: "There he is, right there."

Austin: "Here we go."

Brianna: "Just ignore them and keep walking."

The two walk past a group of about seven kids staring at them.

"Hey crack boy!" shouts Deangelo. Simply his voice makes Austin's heart start to beat rapidly. Austin ignores him and continues to walk. Brianna turns around to look.

Brianna: "They're all following us!"

Austin continues to look forward: "WHAT!?!"

Deangelo: "Hey crack boy! Where are you going?!? We know you don't have a house to go to." The crowd of kids erupts in laughter.

A voice from the crowd: "Yeah, he's a homeless bum on the street!" The crowd laughs again.

Just in front and underneath him, Dineckdin hears laughter, which causes him to look in Austin's and Brianna's direction. He sees a group of kids walking together.

The comment hurts Austin, but he can't let the kids see, so he continues to walk. He has picked up the pace.

Deangelo: "He doesn't have a house cause his Momma burnt it down!"

Austin stopped with his fists clenched, and the crowd behind him also stopped.

Deangelo: "What? What are you gonna do?!?"

Austin looks down at his feet, takes a deep breath, and starts walking again. The crowd starts to follow him again.

Deangelo: "See, that's what I thought!"

Austin's mother always told him not to hit first. She realized while he was at a young age that he had an uncontrollable anger problem. She taught him breathing techniques to overcome the thoughts and help him not resort to violence. That's what he did; he smiled and kept walking. A voice from the crowd says: "He's scared; he's a punk."

Right at that moment, Deangelo rushes forward and pushes Austin from behind, causing him to fall to the wet ground.

Deangelo: "GET UP!"

Brianna jumps into Deangelo's face and pushes him back. "You're just a big show off for your loser friends! Leave us alone and go away!"

Austin gets up and turns around to face Deangelo and the crowd.

Brianna: "You and all of your friends are lame and I'm sick of yall!" She takes off her backpack. "I've been waiting to put hands on yall!"

Austin: "Let's go, Brianna."

Just as he says that, Deangelo pushes Brianna so hard that she goes face-first into a deep puddle of water on the ground. "Shut up!" he says as he pushes her.

Austin rushed up and pushed Deangelo with both hands, causing him to fly backward into the crowd of kids. He then immediately helped Brianna up.

At the sight of her crying, Austin is enraged, and a fire is lit. He turns to the crowd of kids, looks at Deangelo, and begins to take his backpack off.

Austin: "Every day, you choose someone to pick on, and nobody does anything about it. You tripped me, hit me, and pushed me down!"

As Deangelo rushes Austin, you can hear a growl coming from him as he takes a swing. Austin steps to the left and sticks his foot out, tripping and sending Deangelo flying forward and sliding across the sidewalk. The crowd of kids erupts in laughter. Deangelo's hands and ribs were scraped from the concrete. The pain from the scrapes and embarrassment from the kids laughing brought tears to his eyes as he got up even angrier. This time, he walks up with his hands in a fighting stance.

Dineckdins eyes were fixed on the young hero protecting the young female hero. He saw everything and now it was time to see what the young hero could do.

Deangelo swings a right and winces in pain as Austin punches him in his injured ribs at the same time. It hurt so bad that he had no choice but to hold himself in that area.

Brianna screamed: "KICK HIS ASS, AUSTIN!"

Austin fires a left followed by a straight right to Deangelo's face, who is not ready for the combo. This sent him to the ground.

Dineckdin was so happy that he fell off of a tree branch and hit the ground. He quickly climbed back up and continued to watch.

An older gentleman came running up and got in between the two teenagers. As he helped Deangelo up, his eyes were focused on Austin. He asked: "Son, where did you learn how to fight?"

Austin was still angry: "If you're going to tell my mom, make sure you tell her that he started it."

Older man: "Son, I need you to come and meet with me at the Slumberland Gym as soon as you can." With a smile on his face, he says: "You are who I've been waiting for."

The crowd of kids was shocked and stared at Austin. They had no idea that he was capable of what he had just done. As Austin went to Brianna and grabbed his backpack, Brianna whispered: "Do you know who that was?!"

Austin: "No"

Brianna: "That was the great Lenny Litt! He owns the Slumberland Gym. He was an undefeated champ in his time. OH SHIT, Austin, he thinks you're great! You're gonna be the next champ-"

Austin: "Slow down! My Mom is gonna kill me when she finds out I beat someone up again."

Brianna "Again?!"

Austin: "Let's go. Do you think that we can still get free eggrolls?"

Brianna: "Champion fighters DO need food! And Mr. Taos eggrolls are FIRE! You're right, let's go!"

As the two walk away, Dineckdin follows them from a distance. While following, Dineckdin's mind was racing, trying to figure out how he was going to interact with the young hero. Then he had an idea, and he darted past the two while they were talking and walking down the street. There was an old abandoned building on the right side of the sidewalk. He then took out the bracers and buried them under a pile of rubble. He thought to himself, "A cry for help will surely get the attention of a hero. A hero always helps someone in danger." He had to think quickly; he spotted an old door lying against a wall; he grabbed it, pushed it to the ground on top of the pile of rubble, and screamed: "Help!!"

Dineckdin used the voice of the baby hero that he had encountered earlier in the day.

A loud slam followed by a scream stops the two teenagers in their tracks.

Austin: "Did you hear that?!?"

Brianna: "Yeah, that sounded bad!"

Austin: "It came from that abandoned building."

Brianna: "I ain't going in there!"

Austin "Come on!" as he takes off towards the building.

Brianna "Ugh"

As the two get into the building, a cloaked Dineckdin stands by the pile and door that he knocked over. The two teens start looking around to find where the noise came from.

Austin: "Hello?"

Brianna: "Is anyone there?"

Dineckdin lifts the door up and down and says: "Help" again in a childlike voice.

Austin: "Over there under the door!"

He rushes over, lifts the door, then moves wood pieces in a hurry to help the child that he heard. To his surprise, there was no child but a pair of what looked to be old leather gloves with some type of clear crystals attached to them.

Brianna: "What's that?"

Austin: "Just an old pair of gloves."

With the gloves in hand, he looks around to see if the noise came from somewhere else, and then, Dineckdin uncloaks and appears in front of both of the kids. Austin jumps back, and Brianna jumps behind Austin, scared, peeking at the cat-like figure.

Brianna whispers: "What the hell is that?"

Austin: "I have no idea."

Telepathically, Dineckdin says: "Don't be frightened, I am quite peaceful."

Brianna: "Did you just hear what I heard? It talked…"

Austin: "But its mouth didn't move!"

Dineckdin: "I have traveled a long way to find you."

Austin: "Why?"

Dineckdin: "You're a true hero. Your abilities, combined with the bracers, can help me save my planet."

Austin: "PLANET?!"

Brianna: "I knew it; there ARE aliens! I tried to tell people Roswell was real, and they said I needed a tinfoil ha—"

Austin: "Brianna, SHHH!"

Dineckdin: "I'm from Planet Murn, and my people are the Wachooti. Well, there won't be anything left if we don't save them."

Austin: "Wait, do you have a name?"

Dineckdin: "Yes, Dineckdin."

Brianna looks down at her feet and starts repeating: "This is not real, this is not real," several times before Dineckdin walks over and touches her hand.

Brianna, smiling: "Wow, you're like a cat."

Dineckdin smiles back and starts laughing as he did with the baby hero earlier in the day. Brianna laughs as well.

Austin: "What are bracers?"

Dineckdin: "They're in your hands; put them on."

As soon as Austin puts them on, they disappear. "What the?!" Austin exclaimed

Dineckdin smiles and says: "YEESSS! Now you are one with them!"

Austin: "Well, what do they do?"

Dineckdin: "Whatever you believe that you can do."

Brianna: "So you mean he can make a million dollars appear right now-"

Austin: "Brianna, SHH!"

Dineckdin: "What are dollars?"

Brianna: "Din-Din, you have a lot to learn, my hairy friend!"

Austin: "Hmm, so if I wanna..." He grabs the door with both hands and picks it up like it weighs nothing, then throws it into the brick wall, causing it to break into pieces.

Brianna: "WOW!"

Austin: "That's crazy!"

Dineckdin: "Did you believe that you could do that?"

Austin: "Not before today, but HOW!?!"

Din-Din: "It's my invention; I'll tell you all about it on the way to Murn."

Austin: "Wait, MURN? Now? I have to be home in an hour. This is too much for one day!"

Brianna: "Yooo! Let's go to Murn Austin! My mom will be cool with it!"

Austin looks down at Brianna: "How is your mom cool with you going to another planet?!?! Do you even have a mom? We gotta go!"

Brianna: "But what about Din-Din and Planet Murn?"

Austin: "My mom will kill me and Din-Din if I don't get home before dark, and it's getting dark. We gotta figure out how we're going to hide a 4-foot cat that can talk. Can he go to your house? I'm sure your mom won't mind, right?"

Brianna: "Nah, we can't keep him at my house!"

Austin: "Really, now your mom cares?!?"

Dineckdin: "I can hide."

Austin: "How?"

Dineckdin cloaks himself.

Brianna: "That's tiiigggghhht!!"

Austin: "Ok, cool, I guess you're rolling with me." As the three walk off, you can't help but feel a fast friendship on the rise.

Brianna's Story

As the three return to the bus stop, they all decide to part ways and head home. As they split up, Brianna can't help but feel lonely as she starts to walk home. She imagined all of the fun that Austin and Din-Din were going to have. She walks up to her door, puts the key into the lock, and enters.

Her mother is home but sleeping in bed. She works the night shift from 11 p.m. until 7 a.m., so she won't see her daughter until the morning when Brianna leaves for school.

It wasn't always like this, though. Years ago, Brianna's father was in the household. He would always be there to cook meals for Brianna, help her with her homework, and sing songs together while he cooked. Brianna missed her father so much.

Whenever they were all together, it was amazing.

Things went bad, however. Mom and Dad stopped getting along, and they only argued about money. Eventually, her father left.

After he left, the house became cold. There was no more laughter, no more singing, and, worst of all, no more home-cooked meals.

Mom had to work longer hours now, and she was grumpy most of the time. So, Brianna turned to the internet to constantly research things and learn as much as she could about the world. From conspiracy theories to UFOs, Brianna soaked it all up. At one point, she even believed she was telepathic and could move things with her mind.

These days, she's learning about chakras and energy and using affirmations. She's definitely ahead of her peers when it comes to worldly things.

Before her father left, she heard them arguing about her having a brother.

"Maybe that was why he left?"

"He wanted to have a baby boy, but Mom said no."

These are the kind of thoughts she mulled over in her alone time. She also had a lot of alone time due to her mother never being home.

As she laid back on her bed amongst the UFO, posters and drawings splattered on her walls. She couldn't help but wonder what her two new friends were up to.

Austin and Din-Din arrive at Austin's home near dark. As Austin opens the door, his mother approaches and says: "Boy, I was just about to go looking for you; you know what time you're supposed to be in this house!"

Austin says: "Yes, Ma'am, I just got distracted."

Mom says: Yeah, I heard about your little distraction."

Austin: "Wait before you..."

Bonnie: "I heard that you didn't start it and that you were only protecting your little girlfriend."

Austin: "Wait, my lil..."

Bonnie: "Your new trainer for boxing came by, and we talked. I agree that you should get into some kind of sport."

Austin: "Wait, I have a train..."

Bonnie: "I have other news! While you were at school, I found a new place for us to live (with a big smile on her face); you're going to love it!"

Quintan Bizzell

The entire time they were in the kitchen, Din-Din had his eyes on the huge treasure chest that was only ten feet away. He was fantasizing about all of the delicious things that await him when he opens it.

Bonnie: "There's a cleaning crew coming tomorrow morning, and they will be in and out of this place making repairs while we are away. We can expect things to be this way until we move out."

Austin: "So where are we moving to? Is it far?"

Bonnie: "It's just close enough for you still to be able to play with your little girlfriend."

Austin: "Yes! Wait, no! Mom, she's my friend, and she's not even my age!"

Bonnie says with a smile and wink: "I wasn't your father's age either."

Austin, feeling awkward, heads to his room and says: "EWWW!"

Din-Din follows Austin down the hallway.

Austin whispers: "Din-Din, this is where you'll sleep." pointing to the closet. The door was cracked open a bit, and Din-Din could see it was very dark inside. He was scared of the closet.

Austin's left ear started to ring, and he felt scared.

Austin: "Whoa, that was weird. Are you scared, Din-Din? You can stay out here, but you have to be quiet."

Austin didn't know where the ringing came from and thought that maybe it was just a random noise.

As the two settled in Austin's room, he started to think about all of the events from earlier. He thought to himself: "I'm going to be a fighter."

Din-Din says: "You will be the greatest fighter that this planet has ever seen."

Austin sits up in bed: "How did you hear me?!"

Bonnie opens the bedroom door: "Who are you talking to?" she asks.

Austin: "Oh hey, Mom! I was just singing a song."

Bonnie: "Well, it's bedtime; you can sing songs tomorrow."

Austin: "Ok, Mom, goodnight!"

As she closes the door, Austin whispers to Din-Din: "Stop doing that!"

Din-Din says: "I couldn't help but admire your rather large treasure chest."

Austin: "What treasure chest?"

Din-Din: "Does your mother guard it? I can only imagine the many types of treasures you must keep in the..."

Austin: "Hey, go to sleep; there are no treasures...chill."

Din-Din: "What is chill?"

Austin: "Uuugh goodnight"

The alarm clock rings at 7 am.

Din-Din, startled, falls off the dresser he was sleeping on.

Austin wakes up to the thud of Din-Din hitting the floor.

Bonnie rushes into the bedroom to ask if everything is okay.

With a slight grin on his face, Austin says: "Yeah, I'm good; I just fell off the bed."

Clearly very eager, Bonnie says: "Look, today is the day of our fresh start! While you're at school, I will be going over to the new place and then picking up boxes." Trying to make light of the situation, she says: "Well, I guess it's a good thing we had a fire; there's a lot less to move, and Oh, yeah, having your uncles..."

Austin had tuned her out at this point, he was having flashbacks to all the previous times that they had been evicted, and how every time she made it seem exciting, they were starting over.

Bonnie: "And before I forget, your first try-out is today, ok!?"

Austin: "Yes, ma'am."

Austin began to feel anxious, thinking about the tryouts scheduled for later that day. He grabbed his clothes and towel and headed for the shower.

Din-Din sat quietly while he processed the emotions that he felt from the young hero. Din-Din enjoys watching the hero's interactions with other heroes because he gets to feel what the hero feels and learns new words and emotions.

The emotions of Earth people are not like the emotions of the Wachooti people or animals that he's used to. The Wachooti people all kind of feel the same and almost all of them think the same.

On Earth, it's different. Here, everyone is an individual with no limitations on their emotions or thoughts.

And every home has a treasure chest!

"Oh yes" Din-Din thought, as his eyes widened with excitement, he remembered the large treasure chest in the other room.

Austin had just finished his shower and entered the bedroom, just then there was a knock at the front door.

He told Din-Din: "Come on, that's Bri!"

As they walked towards the door, his mother says: "Who are you talking to?"

Austin: "Nobody Mom"

He opens the door, and Bri is standing outside.

Din-Din is quite happy to see her.

As they leave the apartment, Austin says: "Hold on, I'll be right back," as he runs back inside. He grabs a few granola bars and some drinks from the fridge.

He runs out yelling: "Bye, Mom! Have a good day!"

Austin hands out the snacks.

Din-Din takes a bite of the granola bar, wrapper and all. He starts smiling and chewing.

Austin says: "Hey, lemme help you" and he takes the wrapper off and gives the granola bar back to Din-Din.

The look on Din-Din's face when he tastes the granola is like a child seeing fireworks for the first time.

After he tried the drink, you could tell he was in total bliss.

Din-Din says: "I knew you had great discoveries to make inside of your treasure chest!"

Everyone stops talking and looks at Din-Din.

Bri: "Wait, who has a treasure chest?"

Austin: "He keeps going on and on about a treasure chest."

Din-Din: "Ahh, I see. I shall never mention this again (with a big smile)."

Bri: "Hey Din-Din, look as she puts both hands on his shoulders) If you want to be friends, you gotta start using your mouth to speak and stop talking inside of my head! It's weird!"

Din-Din: "Yes, friends, where is my mouth? And what is weird?"

Austin: "Din-Din, you must never show yourself to anyone but us, ok?! It could make other heroes scared."

Din-Din: "Ok? I will not scare heroes."

Austin: "Ok, let's go."

As the three approach the bus stop, Din-Din spots the boys from the fight yesterday and hides behind Austin.

Bri: "Here they come."

Austin: "I know, stay calm."

As the group of boys get closer, they all start speaking to Austin, saying: "Hey" and "What's up?"

As they pass by, Austin cracks a smile.

Bri: "Yeah, yeah! They don't want no smoke from the champ! I thought I was going to have to take off my backpack again!"

At this moment, Austin knew things had changed.

Cho-Goon: "We have rounded up the majority of the slaves on the Planet without any casualties, my Lord. We are ready for Phase 2."

Lord Kull: "No casualties?! Good work. I see that your skills have improved. With results like these, my master will be pleased! I wish to speak to their commanders immediately!"

Cho-Goon: "My Lord, they have no Army."

Lord Kull spins his throne-like chair around, facing towards the stairs where Cho-Goon is standing at the bottom.

Kull stands up and starts slowly walking down the stairs towards Cho-Goon. Kull's presence is intimidating enough to make anyone nervous.

Kull: "Why didn't you just say that from the start? You fool!?" (Kull delivers a straight punch into Cho-Goon's chest, sending him across the shiny floor into the wall).

Kull: "Begin phase two now!"

Cho-Goon jumps up, clutching his chest, and runs out of the door with urgency.

Phase Two, in the process of taking over a planet, is all about preparing newly acquired slaves to begin mining resources. Cho-Goon has an almost flawless ability to sniff out valuable resources in the soil or terrain on any planet.

During this process, he takes a scouting crew and begins looking for resources.

Once found, he sends messengers back to bring slaves and equipment. Once a planet has been depleted, which can take years, the planet is either used for a military installation or destroyed.

Cho-Goon stands at 4ft 7 inches tall with dark brown, almost greyish, colored skin. The facial features of what they would call on Earth a warthog or pig, with two large tusks protruding from his mouth.

The rest of his body, however, is quite human-like.

Very muscular frame with hands that have human-like fingers with five digits.

No one knows his origins except for the fact that he, too, was once a slave to "The Order of On'doon" as a teen.

His home was more than likely destroyed during this very same process that he now commands.

Cho-Goon is known to be a very angry, violent, and sinister creature.

Raised in violence and greed, he proved to have special abilities or a special talent said to be passed down from his now wiped-out species.

He has now climbed the rankings to slave driver and Head of mining operations underneath Lord Kull, with the promise to claim a planet for his own to rule after he completes this mission. He does not seek to disappoint Lord Kull.

Coach: "Double up on that left and follow with the right, Jimmy. Let's go! Yeah, I like what I see! Your opponent can't handle a good, stiff right hand. But we gotta disguise it, Jimmy, so we're gonna overwork the left hand, and as soon as he's comfortable watching for the left, Boom! You're gonna drop the TNT and end the fight! Understand?!"

Jimmy: "Yes, Sir!"

Beep, Beep, beep!

(Electric bell rings to end the round)

Coach: "Next up, stretching, then cardio."

Jimmy "Cardio! Come on, coach!"

Coach: "Do you want to outlast this guy? Maybe if you weren't partying, cardio wouldn't be an issue! There was a time when you didn't question your workout routine; when did you start thinking you were the world champion already? Look At me: Izeez Maldonado has 15 Knockouts, and he's looking to make you his 16th! If you take him lightly and go in unconditioned, he will take you into the later rounds and put you to sleep! All of this neighborhood fame is going to your head. Take the gloves off, start running, and don't stop until I tell you to!"

Jimmy kicks a spit bucket across the floor sending it crashing into the wall.

Coach: "One more slip-up like that, and you can coach yourself, champ!"

School

Din-Din seems amazed at all of the heroes passing by in the hallway of the school. During the walk he smelled something heavenly and stopped in his tracks. Being that Din-Din is invisible, Austin couldn't see him stop and just assumed that Din-Din was still walking beside him.

Din-Din caught up to Austin just in time to walk into the next class. As he sat very closely next to Austin, that heavenly smell drove him insane, and he noticed that the classroom door was still open, so he made his move toward the door.

As he made it to the hallway, he followed his nose down the long hallway. He noticed that the temperature got warmer as he continued, he was then startled by a group of older heroes with funny white hats on. There was lots of steam coming from all areas in this large room, and everything smelled great!

His senses were going wild at this point while trying to figure out how he was going to eat something. All of a sudden, all of the heroes grouped together and walked away. He got excited and immediately began tasting everything in sight! He had never seen so many things to eat in his life!

While moving from location to location in the kitchen eating all that he could, he looked up and spotted four large treasure chests made of a metal-like material; he dropped everything and made his way to them.

The second he touched the handle to open the door, a bell rang, and he heard a door open in the room.

Someone shouted: "What the hell!"

This scared Din-Din

Meanwhile, in the classroom, Austin became overwhelmed with fear and a flash vision of the cafeteria went through his mind.

He thought: "Oh well," and gathered his things to leave the classroom.

A cafeteria cook storms around frantic back and forth in the kitchen yelling as the other workers run over to see what's going on.

Din-Din moves slowly past the scene and makes a run for the door.

Cook: "Some of the kids must've come in and wrecked all of the food that we just prepared. We gotta tell the principal that lunch has to be moved back and check the hallway cameras to see who did this!"

As the crew looks at the mess, they can see that everything that they cooked has been eaten; nothing but stains and crumbs remain.

Running as fast as he can, Din-Din spots Austin and slows down to walk next to him as if he'd been there the entire time.

Austin: "Boy, am I hungry! I'm glad it's lunchtime! I bet you're hungry too, huh Din-Din?"

Din-Din: "Hungry? No, not hungry."

Austin: "Wait, wait, did you say no?!"

Brianna comes running up with a big smile on her face: "Guess what?!"

Austin: "What?!"

Brianna: "I just heard that some kids broke into the cafeteria and stole all the food! (Laughing hysterically) And now we don't have food to eat for lunch. Ha Ha Ha!"

Austin remembered the flash image that happened while he was in the classroom earlier.

Austin: "That's weird."

Briana: "What?"

Austin: "Nothing"

Brianna: "I'm hyped about your tryouts today!"

Austin: "Of course you are; you're not the one fighting!"

Brianna: "You're a great fighter; stop worrying! Besides, there's a reason why I'm not trying out."

Austin: "Why?"

Brianna: "Because my hands are registered as deadly weapons! They call me Gun Show Gonzales!" (staring into the sky)

Austin immediately bursts into laughter

Beeeeeep! (class bell)

Brianna: "Oh shit, we're late, bye!" As she runs to her next class.

Austin: "Din-Din, you've been awfully quiet today; c'mon, let's go."

The rest of the school day winds down and the three are spotted leaving the school to get onto the bus to go home.

While riding on the bus Brianna says: "Hey Austin wanna know where to hit somebody to completely destroy them?"

Austin: "Where?"

Brianna: "Right between the eyes!"

Austin: "Why?"

Brianna: "Because it just destroys them! Everybody knows that! Duh!"

Austin: "That's not true!"

Brianna: "Try it today and see then!"

Austin: "Get outta here!"

As the last stop approaches, everybody slowly gets off the bus.

Briana: "It's time!"

Austin: "I need to stop home and get some shorts and stuff before we head out."

Brianna: "Cool, let's go."

When Austin gets home, the apartment is cleaned out and All of their belongings are gone. His mother comes from the backroom and says: "I got it all in one swoop! We are moved!"

Austin: "Where, though?"

Mom: "1111 Brownberry Lane, apt 3."

Brianna: "That's my building!"

The two both say: "yes!" and high-five each other.

Austin says: "But, hey, I need my..."

Mom: "I put some gym clothes in a bag for you in the kitchen; see you after your practice tonight." She then gives him a kiss on the forehead, and the kids start walking to the gym.

The walk was quicker than normal to the gym, maybe it was because of all the excitement and nervousness built up about the tournament.

As they walk into the front door, they see a few kids that they recognize, but everyone looks nervous.

As soon as they enter, you hear the coach's voice.

Coach: "Alright, alright, everybody, bring it in. You all have been handpicked and referred here by either me or my associates. You are all here to begin the tryouts, earn the right to box in an undercard, and show your skills in the annual Slumberland tournament. So, we will have a mini tournament to see who has what it takes to move to the next level, and we can possibly see your skills, before the Jimmy Richmond vs. Izeez Maldonado fight."

Kid in the back: "Yes!"

Coach: "If you are not here to box, please have a seat on the bleachers. For those who are participating, follow me to the locker room to change and be fitted with gloves and headgear."

Brianna: "You will beat them all."

Austin: "Yeah, I don't know about that."

A large kid walks by, and they look at each other with their mouths open wide.

Brianna: "Yeah, everybody except for that Kid."

All of the boys go back to the locker room, where they change, get weighed, and get gloves and headgear with certain colors.

Coach: "Now that everyone is ready, go down ringside and sit on the bench until your name is called to step up."

Two boys were in the back of the line laughing and goofing off while the coach was talking.

Coach: "Hey!" (to the two boys)

They lookup

Coach: "Repeat what I just said!"

Neither of the boys could repeat what was said.

Coach: "Come to the front of the line; you two are up first!" One of the boys asks, "Who will we fight?"

Coach: "One another to see who goes home."

Everything gets quiet, and all of the boys are seen looking at each other in disbelief.

Coach: "Welcome to Slumberland Gym! We are serious about the sport of boxing and serious about discipline! My name is Lenny, and I'll be showing you the ropes; well, not all of you. Some of you are going home. If you were wondering, yes, I was a world champion. I retired with a record of 34-0-1! I opened up the doors to this gym to give back to the community that supported me. Ok, enough about me; Bert and Ernie are up first! Let's go!"

The two boys hesitated at first but climbed into the ring and took to their corners.

Unseen by anybody else, Din-Din stands up excited and says: "Now I get to see the potential of the bracers!"

Ding Ding Ding!

As the bell rings, the two boys come out and begin throwing blows. You can hear the two assistants on each corner yelling out instructions for the boys to follow.

Coach: "You only get two rounds to show me whatcha got! So, let's go!"

No sooner than the coach got the words out, one of the boys hits the mat and the referee starts counting.

The first match is done.

Coach: "Alright, that's what we came here for! Next up!" (while checking his clipboard)

Austin vs Jeremiah!"

Austin's heart dropped when he saw that Jeremiah was the giant kid that he had seen earlier.

He thought to himself: "How do we weigh the same?"

In the crowd, Brianna whispers: "Oh shit."

Din-Din says: "Yes! oh shit"

As the two boxers face each other from the corners, the bell rings.

Jeremiah immediately advances aggressively and throws a big barrage of punches, leaving Austin with no choice but to block.

Austin's assistant keeps screaming, "Move, "Move! Get outta there!" but he doesn't move.

From the bleachers, you could hear Brianna scream: "Don't just stand there, do something!"

Austin looked terrified.

Noticing that he looked scared, Din-Din focused on Austin. During the relentless barrage of punches, Austin heard: "If you believe, you will win!"

All of a sudden, Austin is hit with A left hook and wakes up out of a daze to a trainer saying, "Moooove!"

He sidesteps to the right and throws a left punch to the body of his opponent. The punch was hard enough for his opponent to shift his body as if he felt it.

As he moves, Austin sent a right hook to the back and sent the young man straight into the corner and a whistle blows. A trainer steps in and says: "this is your first and final warning no punching to the back of an opponent!"

Brianna yells: "Booooo!"

The bell sounds to end the round.

While passing each other, Jeremiah says: "I'm really going to destroy you next round."

Austin sits down on the stool, and his trainer for this round says: "You're quicker than he is! All you have to do is sidestep and deliver shots all day...ok!"

Austin says: "Ok!"

Ding! The second-round bell sounds!

As the two get off of their stools, you can hear whispers. Jimmy Richmond Jr walks by ringside and stops to take in a little action from the youngsters.

While Austin approached the middle of the ring, he heard Din-Din ask: "Do you believe?"

Austin says: "I believe that I can make him stop."

Jeremiah, coming forward full steam with anger in his eyes and the embarrassment from the last round, had something to prove.

Jimmy taps a fellow gym mate and says: "Look, watch this."

As soon As Jeremiah got close enough to swing, Austin ducked down and delivered a punishing blow to the lower rib cage with such force that Jeremiah fell backward onto the mat, screaming in pain and rocking back and forth, clutching his stomach.

Brianna and Din-Din stood up immediately, shocked by the blow.

Din-Din smiles slowly and says: "Yeeaaaas!"

Jimmy couldn't believe what he'd just witnessed.

He's never seen a punch that strong from someone Austin's age.

As the referee counted to ten, Jeremiah was still in pain on the mat. Austin was beginning to understand.

Trainer: "Austin moves to the next round!"

As everyone's hands clapped, Brianna and Din-Din came down to meet Austin as he climbed out of the ring.

Brianna: "Ho Lee shit man! I thought he was going to kill you!"

Austin: "I know! I thought he was too!"

Din-Din: "Now you're getting it. You have to believe!"

As Austin looks over to respond to Din-Din, Jimmy is watching from across the ring. (Austin looks over to an empty seat and appears to be talking to nothing.)

Austin: "You were right, Din-Din!"

Din-Din: "You need more fights to become one with the bracers."

Austin nods his head as they all watch as the matches continue.

"Hey Jimmy" One of the gym mates calls out: "Are you going with us to eat?"

Jimmy is still focused on Austin, and he tells the guys to go ahead because he wants to stay and watch the fights.

While he was watching the others box, he was becoming more and more anxious to see Austin fight again. There was just something about the power behind that punch that left Jimmy intrigued. With only four fights left, it was almost showtime when Coach Litt yelled "Austin, Larry, its Showtime!"

You could hear people whispering and clapping in anticipation of the bout.

Jimmy quickly got up and quietly rushed to the front of the ring next to the coach.

Coach Litt: "What are you still doing here?"

Jimmy: "Just checking out the up-and-coming champs."

Coach Litt: "Mmm hmm, you saw that punch, didn't you?"

Jimmy: "Yes, I did!"

They both kind of chuckled and waited for the previous match to end.

Brianna: "Austin, are you nervous?"

Austin: "Yeah, a little bit; I don't know what to expect."

Brianna: "Well, I've watched this guy's last match, and he's fast, but he's slow, if you know what I mean."

Austin: "Fast, but he's slow?"

Brianna: "Yeah, he's fast, but you can see what he's going to do, so he's slow, get it?"

Austin: "Yeah, I see what you're saying!"

Coach Litt: "Alright, fellas, let's get going!"

Austin's heart started to beat rapidly, as he climbs into the ring he heard Din-Din say "Push the limit of the bracers, you can do it!"

Austin stopped and looked at where Din-Din was sitting. He nodded his head as if he understood.

Jimmy couldn't believe what he just saw. He said out loud but to himself: "I can't believe nobody saw that!?"

Coach Litt: "What did you say?"

Jimmy: "Nothing, Coach, nothing."

Ding Ding Ding!

The match starts, and Larry moves in without hesitation toward Austin.

Impressed by his movement, Austin got hit with two jabs to the face and quickly realized that this guy was faster than he had originally thought.

Austin thought to himself: "I'm going to be faster than him" and almost instantly Larry went for a Jab and Austin moved his head back just out of range of Larry's glove.

Austin laughed to himself and thought: "It worked!"

Upset that he missed, Larry came back with three more jabs with blistering speed, and like nothing, Austin dodged every one of them.

Beep!

The bell sounded, ending the round.

Austin sits down. His trainer is no longer there; instead, Coach Litt is in his corner, and he says: "Good job, Austin! But it will be even better when you decide to actually punch! This is called boxing, and it's not about who can duck the best!"

Beeeeep!

Austin: "Yes, Coach!"

As Austin gets up, he thinks to himself: "Now it's time to prove that I have what it takes!"

Larry comes out, not knowing what to throw, so he does the usual. As he throws the first jab, Austin ducks the punch and instantly delivers a punishing right straight.

Coach Litt: "Yeah, there we go!"

Every punch that Larry threw was unsuccessful and followed with a powerful counter.

This continued for the rest of the second round.

Beeeep! The second-round ends.

Coach Litt: "You are doing great! You have him where you want him now! When will you finish him?"

Austin: "Huh?"

Coach Litt: "Yeah, finish him, put him on the mat, let's go! Show me what kind of power you got in there!"

Austin: "Yes, Coach!"

Beeeeep!

As the third round starts, Austin notices that Larry isn't coming out of his corner. His trainer throws a white towel on the mat and says he's had enough, the bell sounds.

Austin: "Yes!"

While everyone was excited about the match, Austin noticed that Larry was being helped out of the ring by two trainers and looked in bad shape. The coach sees this and comes over and pats Austin on the shoulder and says: "Don't worry about him; he'll be just fine after he heals." (in Austin's ear)

Jimmy sees the Coach whispering to Austin and becomes enraged inside. He grabs his bag and storms out of the gym.

Coach Litt: "Well it's official! Austin Jones will be the main undercard representing Slumberland Gym for the upcoming Jimmy Richmond vs Izeez Maldonado fight. Thanks to everyone who participated and we will continue to work, see you all tomorrow!"

Brianna: "You did it, man! You made it to the big dance now! (while dancing)"

Austin: "That felt great! I'm hungry!"

Brianna: "We should definitely stop by Mr. Taos for a few of dem fire eggrolls!"

Austin: "Bet where's Din-Din?"

Din-Din: "I'm here" (uncloaking)

Austin and Brianna both say: "Hey!" (while blocking him from being seen) as he cloaks himself again.

Austin: "Stop doing that; what did we discuss?"

While walking away from the gym and talking, the three hear someone say: "Hey, Austin! Wait up!"

As the three turn around, everybody's eyes get wider as they notice who it is.

Brianna elbows Austin and says: "Holy shit, that's Jimmy Richmond."

Austin: "Wait who?"

Brianna: "You can't be this..."

Austin: "Oh yeah...oh shit!"

As Din-Din spots Jimmy, he gets scared and immediately moves towards Austin very close.

Austin feels a wave of fear settle over him as Din-Din touches him.

Jimmy: (clapping hands together) "Impressive performance in there. I'm a fan."

Austin: "Thanks, Jimmy!" (with a smile)

Jimmy: "Where did you learn how to punch like that?"

Brianna: "He has raw talent just like you, Jimmy, and he's going to be next up to hold the belt!"

Jimmy: "Is that so?"

Brianna: "No question; with me coaching him and you giving us pointers, anything is possible..."

Jimmy: "Looks like he already has some coaching going on. Who were you talking to in the empty seat? And who were you receiving orders from in the ring?"

A crowd was starting to gather around once they all saw Jimmy.

Austin: "What are you talking about?!"

Jimmy: "Look, I saw you, so there's no need to lie!"

Din-Din and Brianna noticed that the energy had changed in the conversation and began to back away.

Jimmy quietly whispers: "Where's the little cat creature?" Austin's heart starts racing

Austin: "Creature? You must have me mixed up with somebody el..."

Jimmy pushes Austin to the ground and says: "Take them off! They're mine!"

At this point, a nice-sized crowd had gathered around to see what would happen next.

While walking a parent outside to the front door, Coach Litt sees the crowd and starts to approach.

Austin is left on the ground terrified looking up at what everyone deemed as the best boxer in the state and the world.

Jimmy walks over, takes his duffle bag off his shoulder, and drops it on the ground. As he moves to take his shirt off, he says: "Cool. You wanna play dumb, then I guess I'll have to beat them off of you!"

Jimmy starts to walk toward Austin; Austin jumps up and puts up both hands to defend himself.

Jimmy: "Oh, now you wanna rumble with the champ! This is your last warning to take them off!"

(As he clenched his fist and put his guard up)

Austin: "I don't want to F…"

A right hand from Jimmy landed so fast that Austin didn't get to see it coming; he stumbled from the punch.

The crowd went wild.

Jimmy: "Take them off, Austin!" (as he approached again)

As Austin gained his composure, he was hit with a left-right combo to the stomach, followed by an enormously fast straight punch that sent him back to the ground in great pain this time, but Austin thought to himself: "I thought he would hit harder than that, how does he know about the bracers?" Out of nowhere, Coach Litt screams: "What the hell is going on?"

Jimmy: "Your new prodigy stole something that belongs to me, and I want it back!"

Austin: "I didn't steal anything!" (still on the ground)

Jimmy: "Don't be fooled! Nobody punches like that! And that thing from outer space is helping him, I know it! (Brianna's eyes widened as she put her hand over her mouth) He's a cheater and a thief, and I'm going to set the record straight today!"

He starts running after finishing the sentence and kicks Austin in the ribs with enough force to lift him off of the ground.

Austin thought to himself: "Wow, that one hurt, though; I have to do something before he kills me."

Coach Litt screams: "That's it! I have dealt with far too much from you, and you seem to be getting worse! As of today, you are no longer a member of Slumberland gym!"

Din-Din to Austin: "Do you still believe?"

Austin: "He's a champion."

Din-Din: "So are you! Get up and defeat the evil hero!"

Jimmy to Coach Litt: "Ok, fine! Do you think that I care that you kicked me out of a failing gym that can't even make enough money to keep the doors open? Please, you're a washed up has been! I'm the future of Boxing! I am the best that this town has ever seen. Come next week, when your tournament fails because I'm not there to carry you, the doors will be locked for good! Who knows, maybe I'll buy it and…"

Coach Litt moves towards Jimmy with his fist clenched, and a hand on his shoulder stops him mid-stride. It was Austin.

Austin: "I'll take care of this." (As A trail of blood runs down from his nose)

Jimmy: "Get outta the way, old man!" You ready to take them off?!"

Austin: "Come take 'em!"

As the two square up and begin circling each other, Austin imagines not getting hit anymore by Jimmy.

Jimmy swung a right hook, and Austin moved as it barely missed him.

Brianna screams: "That's how you do it!"

Jimmy moves as if he's going to swing again, and Austin ducks. Then Jimmy combines a left and right after the fake, both landing, showing Austin that it wasn't so easy.

You can hear the oooohs coming from the crowd as they reacted to the punches.

Austin shakes it off and moves forward, throwing a left-right combo of his own that lands on the champ. This surprises Austin, giving him more confidence.

Din-Din says: "Yeees! Now, push the limits of the bracers! Believe!"

Din-Din to Brianna: "He He He, his vibration is rising now!"

Brianna: "Huh? He's doing what?"

Jimmy was knocked back a couple of steps from the two punches, touched his jaw, nodded, and said, "That's what I was waiting for."

The crowd silenced when Jimmy stumbled backward

Austin: "There's plenty more if you want seconds!"

Jimmy let out a growl as both fighters sprang forward, and both swung a right at the same time.

A bright flash of light engulfed the two fighters and everyone within viewing range of the fight.

From Austin's view, it was like time stopped. He couldn't move anything but his eyes to look at the surroundings. Jimmy's fist was so close to his face that he could feel the heat coming from his knuckles.

Austin's fist was planted into the forehead right between the eyes of Jimmy, whose face appeared to be dented in by the punch.

The closest people to the action all had their mouths open, and eyes widened as if they were freaked out to see Jimmy's skeleton surrounded by electricity like an X-ray.

A view of the Earth from a distant satellite shows a bright light as if an explosion had occurred.

The flash disappears, and Jimmy flies back almost 15 Ft away, sliding on his buttocks and rolling over to his back, lying motionless.

Din-Din: "He is the one! It is time!"

Brianna runs over to Austin.

Brianna: "How did you do that?"

Austin: "I have no idea, but if he gets up, I'm going to do it again!"

They both look in Jimmy's direction to see people trying to wake him up.

Brianna: "Is he de..."

A loud shriek came out of Jimmy as he sat up, clutching his head with both hands. He kept screaming repeatedly, and people started backing away from him. He finally stopped screaming and stood up. He ran over to his gym bag while never taking his eyes off of Austin, picked it up, and ran away as fast as he could.

He was terrified, and so was everyone else who had witnessed what had just happened.

Din-Din: "You are a true hero!"

Austin: "Do I look like a hero to these people? They look scared of me!"

Din-Din: "You have great power that they do not understand." Brianna hands Austin his backpack.

Brianna: "I told you to hit a man between the eyes to destroy them!"

Austin: "You know what? You were right!"

They both burst into laughter as Austin wipes the blood from his nose and mouth.

As they leave the scene, Din-Din says: "They will never forget this day that you became the greatest hero they've ever seen! I must prepare the ship!"

The Hunt for The Energy Signal

Planet Murn

A dull, repetitive beep echoes from the cockpit of the main ship that Lord Kull commands. Lord Kull was not aboard the ship at this time; he was busy with a group of elders whom he had rounded up for answers.

Lord Kull: "Are these the all-knowing elders that everyone's been whispering about?"

Soldier: "Yes, sir!" (with a snarl)

Lord Kull: "Which one of you is the leader?" None of the Wachooti elders moved or spoke.

Lord Kull: "Ok, nobody wants to talk!"

He grabs the elder closest to him with his left hand, picks him up by the front of his robe, and says: "Maybe you want to talk!"

The elder looks to be trembling, but he doesn't say anything. Lord Kull lets out an angry growl, lifts him higher, and punches the elder in the chest, sending him flying away screaming.

Lord Kull: "Go get him and bring him back; I'm just getting started. I am going to break every bone in all of your pathetic bodies until I get the answers that I seek."

All the elders started to panic because they truly had no answers.

They had no army or generals. They didn't even have anyone trained to fight, so they knew that they were going to be tortured to death.

Just as he reaches for another Wachooti elder,

Cho-Goon says: "My lord, we have made a major discovery! We have hit a large deposit of Wachootium. We have started excavation, but I am requesting more workers."

Lord Kull: "Good work" (while dropping the Wachooti elder)

As he went to pat Cho-Goon on the shoulder, A voice came from behind Lord Kull.

"Lord Kull, your ship is making weird sounds."

Lord Kull smiles as he kicks the Wachooti elder and laughs while heading to his ship. (sending the elder spinning)

Before he gets too far, he says: "Take what you think is necessary to begin maximum overhaul, we are off to a great start!"

Cho-Goon: "Yes, my lord."

Then he belts out: "You heard him! Grab as many hands as you can see with your ridiculously stupid-looking eyes!". He swings an electrified whip and cracks it right down the middle of the nearest soldier's back, shocking him to the point of screaming.

Lord Kull's background is shrouded in mystery. Nobody knows where exactly he came from or how he climbed the ranks of the "Order of On'doon," but one thing's for sure: he is one of the evilest, angriest, and most sinister individuals anyone has ever witnessed.

The history of his reptilian race is the stuff of legend. According to legend, there are multiple reptilian races, some giants, some average-sized. Lord Kull stands 10 feet tall with a very muscular structure.

There was once a legend of a reptilian race of giants living below the surface of Earth. They lived alongside humans and protected them. There was also another race of reptilians that fed on the human race and every other race: predators!

Whatever the case, no one knows which one Lord Kull is connected to. All we know is that he holds a high ranking in the "Order of On'doon" and thrives on power, destruction, and greed.

Lord Kull, now the leader of the "Dark Army" and the head of the table of the "Order of On'doon" has his sights set on Planet Murn.

Lord Kull is equipped with the Dark Army, which is said to be an army of replicated reptilian-like soldiers who operate and think in a hive-mind mentality.

Within the Dark Army, no soldier is unique; every soldier looks the same and shares the same thoughts.

Their voices even sound the same. It was said that the race of clones derived from Master On'doon's pet lizard, which he loved dearly.

The Dark Army, as they are called, does not think; they only carry out orders, which can be a flaw in having a critical thinking strategy. They often die from making simple mistakes because they were only created to take orders. They're physically strong and capable of using brute force to accomplish the mission, but unfortunately, that's all they know how to do.

To everyone, Master On'doon is a mystery. No one knows where he comes from or what he is.

Most who have encountered him have only witnessed his holographic projection and received orders. He appears to be tall, at least 6 feet. He is always seen with a cloak and a hood hiding his body and face. What's seen is a long beak of a nose protruding from a hooded face with glowing eyes. Some say that his eyes light up green when he is pleased with you, and when he is displeased or angry, they glow red. And you can feel the anger.

Some praise him as a scientist and follow him religiously. In contrast, others view him as a murderer and planet killer due to his survival of the fittest mentality while hoarding resources and destroying worlds along his path.

His love for gene splicing and creating new species from every race of people he encounters doesn't get much attention.

It was once said that he possesses a library of every species in the universe and possibly beyond.

*Alarm sounding *

Lord Kull is seen moving quickly to the cockpit of the ship he arrived on

Cho-Goon arrives swiftly behind Lord Kull and says: "My Lord, this deposit is enormously bigger than I stated previously, I believe that I will need A substa..."

Lord Kull: "Quiet! I have never seen energy readings this strong! I must locate where this is coming from. I can only imagine what this could mean for our fleet! The Master will be pleased with this new discovery! Let's pinpoint the exact location and set a course. Make sure that our army continues to mine the precious Wachutium. All hands-on deck!! You and I will be taking a trip to discover this energy reading; ready the ship while I hail our great master!"

Cho-Goon "Yes, my lord."

As Cho-Goon quickly leaves the ship, Lord Kull presses a few buttons in the cockpit that pull up a giant map of planets. He is very focused as he moves from planet to planet, searching for this energy signal. Once he thinks he's found it, he zooms in furiously, only to find out that he was wrong. Bumping into mostly volcanic eruptions and Earthquake seismic activity, He finally gets frustrated and gets up.

Pacing back and forth while looking at a map of a star system. As he sits back down, He spots a planet with many strong energy signals, but one stands out; it turns out to be nothing seismic but primarily electromagnetic.

He gets excited.

He's found the energy is stronger than everything he viewed previously. The planet is mysterious and has lots of water. Now that he's found the location, it's time to contact Master On'Doon. He hits a button that closes and locks the cockpit door, and he pushes a button on a holographic communication device to hail Master On'Doon. As he releases the button, a hooded figure appears before Lord Kull.

Lord Kull: "Massssster!"

On'Doon: "I expect that you have good news!"

Kull: "Yes, mining is going as planned, and there is no pushback from the creatures here."

On'Doon: "Good, how many casualties?"

Kull: "None"

On'Doon: "None?! Like taking jarilax from a giglaar!"

Kull: "Exactly."

On'Doon: "Then why do you disturb me with small talk!?"

Kull: "Master, I am requesting permission to pursue a large energy reading off the planet while continuing to mine here."

On'Doon: "Absolutely not. You will stay in position until at least 50% of the resources have been gathered! Until then, I expect samples of every species of life on the planet. By the way, your first quarter check-in is almost due." (the hologram disappears)

Lord Kull stands up abruptly, turns around, and screams as he hits the door with both hands (during the scream, the electronic click happens again)

On'Doon screams: "Kull!"

Scared out of his rage, Lord Kull straightens up and says: "Yes, Master."

On'Doon: "Do we have a problem?"

Lord Kull: "No master"

On'Doon: "Good, get back to work"

Lord Kull: "Yes, master" (with a long hiss)

As the projection disappears, Lord Kull turns, hits the button to open the door, and Cho-Goon falls at his feet.

It appears that he was eavesdropping on the meeting with On'Doon. Lord Kull lets out a long growl.

Cho-Goon: "My lord, I know what it loo.."

Lord Kull kicks Cho-Goon so hard that he squeals while sliding across the ship's starboard side.

Lord Kull: "Now Get up! Go and set mining operations to autopilot, begin the collection of samples with the lab crew, and when that's done, ready the ship. We have a new mission!"

Cho-Goon: "I'm sure Master On'Doon will be pleased with…"

Lord Kull balls up his fist and approaches Cho-Goon

Lord Kull: "You fool! I've conquered hundreds of planets! Do you think that came by way of rules? I AM the Great Lord Kull! Now, ready the ship before I break you in half!"

Cho-Goon jumps up and begins following orders immediately. Lord Kull punches in the coordinates of the energy signal to get ready to take off.

As Cho-Goon leaves to begin giving orders to the soldiers, Lord Kull sits back and stares at the map display before him. You can feel the greed growing by the second as he imagines finding this significant energy signal. Harvesting energy is the driving force behind the Dark Army's ability to expand resources to power their space fleet, along with capturing and enslaving every species from every Planet that they invade, ensuring that the machine lives on. The Dark Army consists of 100 percent nomads and mercenaries. They have no home planet; they live in space, and they sit and wait for orders while scanning whatever planets are local to them wherever they are. Scanning local planets is how the Dark Army discovered Planet Murn.

Lord Kull noticed a resource or mineral that was foreign and decided to invade the planet to find this unknown resource to please Master On'Doon.

Cho-Goon: "My Lord!"

This startled Lord Kull and woke him up. He had fallen asleep fantasizing about the energy source.

"We are ready for departure!"

Lord Kull: "It's about time. Let's go!"

As the thrusters ignite and the ship rises, you can see the fires and smoke coming from what once was a place of peace and happiness in the backdrop, slowly fading into the darkness of space.

Din-Din's Quest

Austin lay in his bed, tossing and turning, thinking about the events of the previous days. He heard the phone ring. His mother answered, saying: "Hello, Coach Litt."

Austin's heart started racing instantly.

Bonnie: "Oh no! Are you serious?! Is everything ok?! He did? Well, I don't know what to say! We will definitely have a sit down to figure out the best course of action. I'm sorry to hear that! I will keep everyone in my prayers! I hope things get better. Ok, Coach, goodbye."

By this time, Austin is freaking out, and he keeps saying to himself: "I'm dead, I'm dead. She is going to kill me; I'm dead."

A few moments later, Austin hears his name being called in the living room.

As he walks into the living room, he realizes that his mother is actually in her room. It's only been two days in their new apartment, so he sometimes gets confused.

Bonnie: "We need to have a talk."

Austin: "Before you say anything, I did not mean to hit him that hard."

Bonnie: "Well, however, you hit him, the coach seems to think that you have great talent."

Austin: Huh?"

Bonnie: "Yeah, but I have some bad news."

Austin: "Wait, we saw him get up. I didn't kill him!"

Bonnie: "Austin, will you calm down? Nobody said you killed anyone!"

Austin: "Wait, so he's not dead?"

Bonnie: "Who's not Dead?"

Austin: "Yes! Wait, so what's the bad news?"

Bonnie: "Your coach is closing the gym for good. He wanted me to tell you that you were a great listener and someday you will be a great fighter, but he can no longer teach you. He told me the name of another gym his friend owns if you want to continue boxing. I know this is a lot to take in right now, so think about it and let me know later. Ok?"

Looking confused, Austin says: "Ok." and returns to his room.

As he enters his room, he finds Din-Din uncloaked and pacing back and forth.

Austin: "I can see you. Are you crazy?"

Din-Din: "All I need to do is find out what's shorting out the propulsion systems."

Austin: "What?"

Din-Din: "I need to fix the ship."

Austin: "Where is it?"

Din-Din: "Where I met the evil hero."

Austin: "You met Jimmy. That's how he knew I had the bracers and tried to kill me. Wow, thanks for the heads-up!"

Din-Din: "What's heads up?"

Austin: "Uugh, never mind, man!"

Din-Din: "When the sun comes back, I will begin the mission of repairing our ship."

Austin: "Our ship?"

Din-Din: "My planet needs us! They will all be killed!"

Bonnie yells from down the hall: "Who tried to kill you?!"

Austin: "Nobody, Mom, I was just singing a song!"

Bonnie: "I told you about those types of songs! Not in my house!"

Austin: "Yes, Maam!" (as he looks at Din-Din with his fingers over his mouth, telling him to be quiet)

Austin: "Talk in my head."

Din-Din: "You said not to."

Austin: "Just do it!" (while whispering)

Bonnie: "Oh yeah, make sure that I have all of your dirty laundry, Austin! I'm doing laundry tomorrow, and I know how you love to keep dirty clothes!"

Austin: "Yes, Mom!"

Bonnie: "You should see the laundry room here. It's very clean and nothing like the last place."

Austin thought the entire apartment building was nicer than the last several they had lived in. There were no drug addicts walking around like zombies. The hallways didn't smell like urine, and oh yeah, Brianna lives here, too! A smile came over his face, and Din-Din asked: "Where's the little hero?"

Austin: "That's a good question."

It's Friday, and all of the madness happened on Thursday at the gym. Austin hasn't heard from Brianna since the tournament.

Din-Din: "That's it!"

A loud ringing in the right ear of Austin catches his attention.

Austin: "What?"

Din-Din: "It seems like the electromagnetic pull from the planet affected the gyroscope and gravitic resistance, causing a power interference; AHHH, yes! And now I can repair the system! I must begin now!"

Austin: "Now?!"

Din-Din: "Yes, I must go!"

They both stand looking at each other.

Austin: "Well, my mom's in the kitchen, so…"

Din-Din: "But I must…"

Austin runs to the window and opens it.

Din-Din: "I will return!"

As Din-Din goes to climb out of the window, Austin's mother calls out.

Bonnie: "Hey, are you dressed? Coming in!"

Austin's eyes grow large as he quickly runs to the window and hurries Din-Din out to the ledge. He shut the window and blinds just as his mother opened his bedroom door.

Austin: "Hey mom...Sup?"

Bonnie: "Don't sup me, I'm not one of your friends. Gather your laundry and get ready to come with me to our fabulous new laundry room, I was gonna wait but..."

Austin: "But mom I..."

Bonnie: "Or you can clean this room and the rest of the house until I get back!" With a smile.

Austin: "OK, OK!"

Bonnie: "I know, I know. And take everything out of your pockets this time!"

As Austin moves to begin collecting his dirty clothes outside the window, Din-Din is hanging onto the ledge with one finger, and he's slowly slipping. He's five floors up, and he has no more strength to hang on. As his finger gives way, he calls out to Austin telepathically.

Austin: "What the..." he stands up

As he sees a vision of Din-Din falling, he rushes to the window but finds nothing.

Din-Din falls four floors down into a dumpster in the back of the building. Pretty banged up, he was very thankful that something broke his fall. As he climbs out of one of a row of dumpsters, he shakes it off and remembers what he set out to do. He smiles and starts walking in the wrong direction to get the ship.

Cho-Goon stares blankly into the darkness while navigating the E-shuttle to get to their target. In the dead quiet, you can hear the soft chirps and beeps coming from the ship's navigation system.

Lord Kull: "How long do we have?"

Cho-Goon: "We are about fifty percent to our target, my Lord."

Lord Kull: "Good. I would like to make this quick. Move into warp speed to cut down on time!"

Cho-Goon: "My Lord, we cannot go any faster"

Lord Kull: "And why is that?!"

Cho-Goon: "Upon readying the ship, I removed all items that would have weighed us down and slowed our travel."

Lord Kull: "You mindless giglaar! Did you dump our fuel cells to go faster? Now we can't go into warp speed, and we could run out of fuel?!"

He stands up and approaches Cho-Goon.

Cho-Goon: "Please forgive me, my Lo..."

Lord Kull lifts him out of his seat with his left arm and starts punching him repetitively in the stomach with his right hand and saying things in his native language.

Chandra: "Sweetheart, can you hand me the detergent from over there?"

Brianna: "How long do we have to be here? I wanna go play with my friends!"

Chandra: "I only had a few days off to run errands and get all of this laundry done. Just a little while longer, and I promise you can hang out with your friends once we're finished. We'll have a nice clean house and fresh laundry. I've noticed that you've been spending a lot of time with your new friends. Who are they?"

Brianna: "Well, we hang out at school. We ride the bus together."

Chandra: "Oh yeah, sounds like fun."

Brianna: "Out of this world fun Mom."

Chandra: "Nothing like having a good group of girls to grow up with and share experiences with. I miss those days; they are girls, right?"

Brianna: "Well, his name is Austin, and my other friend is Din-Din."

Chandra: "Brianna, we had a long discussion about why you shouldn't be having a boyfriend at your age."

Brianna: "EEEEW Mom they're my friends, that's it! You'll see because Austin just moved into our building."

Chandra: "Wait, what? In our building?"

Just as the two are talking, Austin hurries into the Laundromat carrying a basket and places it next to a washing machine.

Brianna: "Hey man! We were just talking about you! Mom, this is Austin, Austin. This is my mom, Chandra."

Austin: "Hey! nice to meet you, I gotta go help my mom or she'll kill me!"

Everyone laughs as Austin bolts out the door.

Din-Din has been walking for quite some time now, and he's starting to feel like he doesn't recognize anything. What he does recognize is the smell of hero food that seems to be creeping out of every house and building as he walks along a main street.

Just up the street, he saw heroes lined up, and it appeared that they were getting food handed to them. So, he hurried to the line to see what was going on. As he got closer, he realized that what he thought was true. He watched as a large hero and a child hero walked up to a window and smiled as they got food from a hero with a big white hat on.

Din-Din went to the side of the rather small hut and climbed up to peek inside. Inside the hut was A rather large hero making food and a normal-sized hero putting food into a container. At that moment, he heard:

Cook 2: "Alright, Number 43, one large gyro, fries, and drink!"

Din-Din thought: "Finally, this is where to get hero food, and it's called Heroes! If I get in line, then they will give me some of that delicious hero food!" Then he thought: "Wait, I can't reveal myself to the other heroes. I promised Austin that I would not scare them."

So, he sat there trying to figure out how to get some.

Austin and his mother carried in the rest of their baskets, and Brianna was there waiting to help.

Brianna whispers: "Hey, Austin. What have you guys been up to?"

Austin whispers: "Nothing much. I've been stuck in the house with my mom, and now she's got me here."

Brianna: "Man, me too! My mom won't let me leave until we finish the laundry. Where's Din-Din?"

Austin: "I have no idea."

Brianna: "What?!" in her normal voice.

Austin: "Shhh! (while looking around) He has been going crazy about fixing his ship. He said he figured it out and left."

Brianna: "Noooo! Man, you can't just let him wander the streets, MAN!"

Austin: "Well, what was I supposed to do? Trap him in my closet?"

Brianna: "Yes! That's exactly what I would've done!"

Austin: "You are definitely special."

Brianna: "Thanks. My Dad used to tell me that all the time."

As the kids have a recap of all of the events quietly at a nearby table, Austin's mother, Bonnie, goes over to the change machine to get quarters for the laundry.

When she gets there, Chandra, Brianna's mother, repeatedly puts a dollar bill into the machine.

Chandra: "Ugh, this stupid machine won't take this dollar!"

Bonnie: "Let me give it a try (with a smile)."

Chandra: "Good luck!" (as she hands her the one-dollar bill)

On the first try, Bonnie gets the machine to accept the dollar.

Shonda: "Wow, if only you knew how long I've been fighting that evil machine; thank you! I'm sorry, what's your name? I'm Chandra, and my little Brianna is at the table."

Bonnie: "Oh, you're Brianna's mother. Finally, I get to meet you. Well, you probably already know that's my son Austin."

Chandra: "Yes, I've heard so much about him."

Bonnie: "Did you hear that he gets on my nerves?"

The two women share a chuckle and get back to their laundry.

As Bonnie returns to loading the laundry into the washer, she looks at Chandra sneakily.

She recognizes her face but can't quite remember where it came from.

Din-Din has exhausted all options on how to get hero food and is now in a trance, somewhat hypnotized by the huge chunk of meat spinning and dripping juices in front of him on the other side of the glass. He can smell it to the point of tasting it, and he can no longer take it. Then he thought, "Yes! I will take it!"

Then the cook yells

Cook #2: "OK, OK, #51, one extra-large gyro, extra everything, fries, and a ..."

As he puts the bag out of the window, it is snatched and floats off at a high rate of speed down the street and into an alley.

Cook #2: "Hey! What the!"

Din-Din had snatched the sandwich and was now on the run at top speed. Not knowing where to go, but looking for a safe place to hide and eat his hero food. As he sprinted through the alleyway, a group of teens were recording themselves doing tricks on their bicycles.

Teen #1: "Hey, whoa, look!"

All of the teens focus their cellphone cameras on a food package zooming by the garage.

Teen #1: "Shhh, come on!"

He motions for everyone to follow the package. About 6 of the 7 teenagers follow him with the cameras still focused and recording.

Din-Din finally finds a safe place on the side of a garage to stop. All that he can think about is eating. He unwraps the food and can't believe his eyes. It's beautiful. There was so much meat and sauce and little yellow sticks that complimented the meat so well, He was in heaven.

About halfway through his meal he heard a few footsteps, he quickly turned around. There was a young hero looking in his direction as if he could see him. The young hero kept coming closer leaving Din-Din scared. As soon as the young hero reached down to touch his hero's food, Din-Din uncloaked and let out a shriek.

Right at that moment all of the teens appeared with their cameras. Din-Din began running and they all tripped over each other trying to escape whatever it was that just appeared.

After running for so many blocks, Din-Din slows down. With his heart racing, he stops to breathe. He could hear the sound of running water to his left; he turned to look to find an older hero staring directly at him, holding a long tube that was pouring water on the ground. The older hero looked frightened. Din-Din remembered that he was uncloaked and immediately cloaked himself and began walking. He noticed a sign that said Lakefront with a water symbol. He remembered seeing that sign when he landed.

He then thought: "That's where my ship is!" and began running again.

Brianna: "So you just let Din-Din jump out of the window and run free, I don't like that idea, it could get real gangsta for our furry little outer space friend."

Austin: "I know but I couldn't stop him, he was pretty determined to fix the ship."

Brianna: "Yeah so what happens when he fixes the ship?"

Austin: "I dont know."

Brianna: "What do you mean you don't know? We have to save his people Austin!"

Austin: "Whoa, hey wait a minute. Did you think about what if we die? What if we can't get back home? What if we get kidnapped and turned into slaves of some alien race? What if they eat us?!"

Brianna: "Shhh!"

The two teens watch as Bonnie approaches Chandra

Bonnie: "Excuse me Ms. Chandra, I have a question."

Chandra: "Sure"

Bonnie: "Do you know Johnny?"

Chandra: "Johnny who?"

Bonnie: "Johnny Jones, they call him JJ for short. He makes music, JJ and the Wonders?"

Chandra: "Sounds like you're referring to Brianna's father Johnny Jones, why?"

Bonnie's face went pale and Austin looked down at his feet in disbelief.

Bonnie: "So I finally get to lay eyes on the woman that my husband left his family for!"

Everything got quiet

Bonnie: "And you have a child together, how old is she?"

Austin: "Mom!"

Bonnie: "How did you meet? When did you meet? Did you know he had a family?"

Chandra: "I never knew anything about you; I only knew that he had a son."

As all eyes move towards Austin

Chandra: "Well, Brianna, say hello to your brother, whom I begged your father to let you meet."

Brianna: "What the Fuck!?"

Chandra: "Brianna!"

Brianna: "I'm sorry, Mom (as she walks out of the laundromat). I need a minute."

Bonnie: "Austin let's go!"

Austin: "Yes ma'am!"

Quintan Bizzell

He's Here

It has been about an hour now, and Din-Din has walked the streets near the lake front looking for something familiar to jog his memory of where he left his ship. He finally gets a glimpse of water and things start to look like he remembered the night that he crash landed in the water. There was only one problem, the entire area looked the same and each section felt the same. Except for one area that he could see that was about a mile ahead, it was where he met the evil hero. He picked up speed now that he knew the exact location.

Cho-Goon: "We are now about to enter the planet's orbit and soon the upper atmosphere."

Lord Kull: "It's about time! I will need you to put a visual up as soon as possible, I want to know all about the species here on this planet!"

Cho-Goon: "Yes, my lord!"

(A couple of seconds go by)

A visual of the planet is now loading my lord!"

Lord Kull swings his chair around to get a good look at the screen.

Lord Kull: "Mmm, bigger than expected, I bet it's crawling with resources" (with a smile)

Cho-Goon cackles and says: "I can smell it from here!"

Lord Kull rubs his hands together and says: "Get us closer!"

Austin: "Mom, are you ok?"

Bonnie: "Austin, I've always wondered what the other woman looked like that your father left us for."

Austin: "I know Mom, but it's not her fault, she said that she didn't know."

She looks Austin in the eyes and says: "The side chick always knows that they're the side chick."

Finally, Din-Din makes it to the spot where he left the ship. He looks around to make sure, he's having trouble remembering certain landmarks because it was pitch black when he crashed. He decided that he should just dive into the water and locate the ship. As soon as he hits the water, he lets out a scream of bubbles once he feels how freezing cold the water is. To his surprise after diving deep he realized that the ship was no longer in the place where he remembered. A rush of fear and panic settled in as he took a deep breath and immediately dove back in. This process of Din-Din coming up for air and quickly diving back under to locate the ship went on for a few hours until the sun went down.

Cho-Goon: "My Lord, brace yourself, for there is turbulence ahead. We are entering the planet's atmosphere."

As the small ship begins to rock side to side with lights flickering

Knock! knock! knock!

There was a knock at the door at Austin's apartment. Both Austin and his mother looked shocked because no one knew where they lived. Austin went to the door, thinking: "This must be a mistake; we never get visitors."

As he cracks the door, he sees Brianna. She still looks a little down from what happened at the laundromat earlier that day.

Austin: "Hey, is everything alright?"

Brianna: "Not really, everything is very weird now, but I'm cool. Can you step outside for a moment?"

Austin: "Yeah, yeah lemme let my mom know that it's you at the door."

Austin quickly goes to tell his mother that he's right outside the door and hurries back.

Brianna: "Is she like mad at my mom?"

Austin: "Well to be honest it goes A little deeper than that. She hasn't been really happy since my dad, sorry, our dad left us. I'm sorry that she kinda took it out on your mom today."

Brianna: "Yeah that was a little too much for me and I had to leave."

Austin: "Yeah me too, that was the last thing I expected!"

Brianna: "Learning that you are my brother was really cool, but also very confusing."

Austin: "I know, but I'm happy to find out that you're my sister too."

Brianna: "Where's Din-Din?"

Austin: "I have no clue."

Brianna: "What if he's gone?"

Austin: "I hope not, but what can we do?"

Brianna: "We could go looking for him!"

Austin: "Where?"

Brianna: "Right! Ok, well I guess he doesn't want us to save his planet!"

Austin: "Yeah I guess not."

Brianna: "Well Big Bro, guess it's back to real life."

Austin: "Yeah, wait that was real life?!"

Brianna: "Hey I gotta get home my mom doesn't know that I'm here."

Din-Din lays on the rocks as the waves crash up against the shore. He's completely exhausted from diving and is now resting and breathing.

"Did someone find it and take it? Am I in the wrong area?" He was trying his best to figure out where the ship could've gone.

While thinking and staring at the coastline he noticed that it curved to the left about a hundred yards creating a bight, and he thought right away: "Thats where it is!"

Out of breath he runs to the curve and jumps into the water, excited to discover the ship not far down, close to the bottom of the lakebed. The ship sitting on the bottom amongst all of the tall weeds, swaying back and forth as if there was a breeze blowing under the water.

Now knowing where the ship is, he swims to the surface just to stick his head above the water so that he can breathe. Not wanting to lose sight of the ship, he doesn't go back to the shore. Wondering how he is going to get the ship door opened and closed without letting large amounts of water in. With no solution to this problem, he shrugs his shoulders takes a deep breath and dives down to enter the ship.

He finds the latch button and the door opens; he gets inside and immediately closes the door to find that the ship is almost completely underwater on the inside. Holding his head above water in about a foot of empty space, his only thought was to start the ship and get it out of this water. If it starts.

With fire all around their ship, Cho-Goon and Lord Kull are seen rocking back and forth, up and down as if they were on a rollercoaster.

Cho-Goon: "Not too much longer my Lord, we are very close."

Lord Kull: "Good I'm eager to see what awaits."

Cho-Goon: "This will be like taking Jarilax from a Giglar!"

During his sentence the ship lost all power and slowly began to fall. They were no longer in space, so the ship started to fall faster and faster. The long-lasting fall made the two panic and now they were both screaming. Cho-Goon was screaming from fear And Lord Kull was screaming At Cho-Goon.

At About 1000ft from the surface, Cho-Goon stops screaming, flips open a glass topped red button and holds it down. The power returns and the ship levels itself out and hovers in midair.

As Cho-Goon smiles at the power returning, he heard the sound of a safety harness releasing. As he turns around, he is met with a barrage of punches.

Lord Kull: "You had access to emergency power this entire time?! I am going to destroy you, you lower life form!" while delivering punch after punch.

Din-Din managed to find the ignition button to start the ship, but he had to repeatedly press the button to get it started. It took A few dives until it finally started up. Din-Din lit up with excitement while taking a break to breathe.

He thought to himself: "Now it's time to get this ship out of the water!"

He then took a huge breath and dove down, strapped himself into the seat and lifted the ship out of the water.

In the distance, a couple having dinner at their favorite seafood restaurant on the lakefront is seen holding hands and staring at the moon off of the back deck

Woman: "Arnold this is wonderful!" as she rubs the top of his hand

Arnold: "This view never gets old; it almost looks like the moon is coming out of the water and go… wait what's that?!"

The two see what looks like a sphere or orb shaped object rise out of the water right in front of the moon. It was clear to them that this was something that they've never seen before.

Din-Din successfully raised the ship out of the water. He stopped the ship, unsnapped his safety harnesses, and swam to the exit hatch and pushed the open button causing all of the water to rush out of the ship. If it wasn't for him hanging on to the left door frame of the hatch, he would have been dumped out with the rush of water.

The couple notices that a light turned on in the object that they were viewing in front of the moon, it looked like a door, then something like a creature was seen hanging on for dear life as liquid spilled out of the object. The two were confused and couldn't believe what they were witnessing.

Din-Din, heart racing, pulled himself back up into the ship thanking the elders because he almost lost the ship, runs back to his seat and began activating the cloaking and checking all functions of the ship.

Waiter: "And here's your oysters Rockefeller" he notices that the man and woman are staring at something in the distance and didn't break focus when he brought them their order.

Woman: "It was just there and then it disappeared!"

Waiter: "What disappeared?"

Woman: "The ship!"

Waiter: "Oh yeah, ships come and go all the time down here."

Arnold: "No, it was a spaceship with a little person in it!"

Waiter: "Alll righty then, here's your food, lemme know if there's anything else that I can do for you fine people. I'll be right back with your drinks."

Still reeling from the punches from Lork Kull, Cho-Goon is seen rubbing his hand on what appears to be a budding knot on the top of his head. His eyes widened with wonder once he starts to see blinking lights and structures as the ship begins descending downward through the clouds. Lord Kull gets out of his seat to come closer to the front to view the scenery.

Lord Kull: "Find a place to land immediately!"

Cho-Goon: "Yes my lord, the oxygen levels are quite higher than what we are accustomed to my Lord, so there is no need for our own."

Lord Kull: "This will be the greatest find yet! Once I have conquered it and we begin operations." (with a long hiss)

Cho-Goon: "This will ensure that we will have our own pl..."

Lord Kull: "Shut your muzzle and find a place to land!"

"On most of the planets it would be easy to find a place to land that did not have structures" Cho-Goon thought to himself: "What kind of planet was this where there was a structure on every part of the landscape?"

He decided to find the first place that had a nice open area that the ship would fit then land.

His eyes widened once he starts to see blinking lights and structures as the ship begins descending downward through the clouds.

Din-Din had been hovering over the same spot where he released all of the ships water for several hours now, making sure that each function was still functioning properly before his great return to his home planet. He stopped for a moment to imagine the looks on everyone's faces when he returns to save them from their evil captors. A vision of them carrying him all the way to a throne where he is fed the finest of foods, while getting his feet rubbed came to a startling halt when he heard something hit the craft.

Looking out of the front window he saw winged creatures flying towards the ship, he quickly elevated the ship to a higher altitude for the moment. Only equipped with whatever tools he left in the ship while trying to get it to work back on his home planet, is what he had available to repair his ship now. So, he hopes that the repairs will be easy. He can't help but notice that since finding the ship there hasn't been any signs of anything malfunctioning. As he snaps out of his pondering, he thought: "I must now get back to Murn with Austin" as he decides to head towards the direction he came from and trace his steps.

Sitting in her room with nothing to do, Brianna appears to be bored out of her mind until she hears A knock at her bedroom door.

Knock Knock Knock

The door opens and it's her mother with a smile on her face. This was kinda weird because normally she would be on her way to sleep before heading to work.

Brianna: "OK mom, what's going on?"

Chandra: "Well I know things have been crazy here lately with my work schedule, you being alone a lot and to top it all of what we found out today, I feel that we are kinda losing touch I so ordered this for you"

(she pulls out a brand-new cell phone)

Brianna lets out a scream of joy when she sees her gift.

Chandra: "Now we can stay connected even when I'm not home, plus you can call your newly discovered big brother." (she says with a wink)

Brianna: "Thank you Mom! I love you so much!" She gave her mother the biggest hug and rushed to open the box.

Chandra: "The guy at the phone store said that it's all hooked up so the rest is up to you! I gotta get to bed, oh I had him program my number into your phone. I love you, call me whenever you need to talk."

Brianna powered the phone on to check the battery and play with the phone's features while charging it when she noticed the top stories in the news for the day.

The first story was titled "Kids find Alien in Alley"

She clicked it and began reading the story and realized that this happened fifteen minutes away. As she continued to read to the end, she saw a link that said click here to watch the video, without any hesitation she clicked it. As she watches the video, she sees some kids chasing a floating sandwich and says: "They gotta get better at faking, anybody can put a sandwich on a string." Just as she gets ready to exit the video, she sees Din-Din holding the Sandwich.

Brianna: "Yooo!"

As she plays the video back over and over again you can see the sadness fall over her face. As she wipes a tear from her cheek she says: "He's all alone out there"

As the next video starts to play automatically, a woman's voice says: "We couldn't believe our eyes! We actually saw a ufo with a little person in it!!" "Yeah, like a cat!" A man's voice interrupts the woman, "Right here at our favorite restaurant!"

The camera zooms out to show the restaurant and Brianna says: "Hey I know that place!"

Cho-Goon has found an open area to begin lowering the ship. As the landing legs extend and sounds of pressure releasing begin, the ship comes down slowly and lands.

Lord Kull: "Open the hatch, lets survey the environment."

Cho-Goon: "Yes my lord!"

The hatch opens and the two walk out.

In the distance there is a sign visible that says: "Washington Park".

While they were walking out and the lights from the ship began to dim, they noticed a crowd of life forms approaching.

Voices from the crowd: "Wow, what is that?!" Oh my god, this is crazy!" "It's too dark, I can't get a good picture, nobody's going to believe this!"

Before all of the commotion, A group leaning up against a vehicle were watching the ship land in disbelief.

Guy #1: "We need to have a plan in case something comes out of whatever that is man!"

Guy #2: "You can't plan for that kind of shit!"

Guy #3: "Well what do you suggest we do, oh great leader?!"

Guy #4: "We should rob em; they probably got all types of valuable stuff in that rocket!"

Guy #5: "It's called a spaceship dummy, you know like a UFO!"

As the group starts agreeing, Lord Kull emerges from the lights and dust, walking down the ships landing ramp.

Guy #2: "That's a big mother...."

Guy #4: "Get your guns and let's do this!" (while cocking his gun)

Everyone grabs their guns and follows.

As Lord Kull approaches the herd of life forms, he starts getting energy readings of each individual life form. He saw so many 8's and 11's that he felt that none of them could overpower or hurt him in any way.

During his scanning process about five lifeforms were spotted rushing to the front, pushing and shoving the others to get a closer look.

 Cho-Goon: "They appear to be excited to meet you, my Lord!"

Lord Kull: "Ahhh this will be like taking Jarilax from A Giglar!"

As the group rushes up to the front of the crowd, they all stop abruptly once they get a full visual of the 10ft lizard-like creature staring back at them. The fear that came over the men as they looked into the eyes of Lord Kull could be seen in the facial expressions and body language as they stared back at the giant. Lord Kull stepped forward a couple of steps put his hand onto his chest and says: "I am Lord Kull, I command the Dark Army, I Serve Master On'doon, The ruler of The Order of On'doon!"

Not realizing that to the humans he just roared and growled at different pitches

At the end of his sentence one of the humans fainted and someone screams: "What the!"

Everyone that rushed to the front pulled out guns and started firing at Lord Kull.

Lord Kull shielded his face with his arm and screamed: "Back to the ship!"

As the bullets bounced off of his scaly skin and armor.

Cho-Goon made it to the ship first and turned around and waited for Lord Kull to make it inside and pressed the button to close the hatch.

Lord Kull: "I spoke of peace and was met with war!"

Cho-Goon: "I believe that they did not understand you, my Lord."

Lord Kull: "Nonsense, they are not intelligent enough to reason! Primates!"

Cho-Goon: "Perhaps on our next encounter we will use our ships language modification chips."

Lord Kull: "How long have you known that we've had such tools?" (as he inches closer to Cho-Goon)

Cho-Goon: "We've never had to use them bef..."

Lord Kull begins beating Cho-Goon in his back while Cho-Goon flees to the cockpit of the ship.

Lord Kull: "I've had enough! Retrace the energy signal and set a course immediately, and if you fail, your death will be here on this primitive ignorant planet! Do you understand?" (With his eyes glowing red)

Cho-Goon: "Yes, my Lord!"

Cho-Goon has only seen Lord Kull's eyes glow once before and afterwards he destroyed 30 soldiers in a violent rage. He knew that he couldn't fail this time.

As the ship lifted off, you could still hear gunfire and bullets ricochetting off of the ship and people screaming in the back ground.

While on his way back to Austin's building, Din-Din paid close attention to every sound and every level on the digital screen in front of him, to make sure that nothing failed. The only place to land the ship was on top of Austin's building. This was the perfect place to continue checking and repairing before the journey back to Murn. He's come a long way and he could have died many times on this quest, as he thought to himself: "I'm going to be a hero, a hero to my people!"

He had just made it to the top of the building and began to set the craft down on top of the roof. Brianna paced back and forth in her room trying to build up the nerves to sneak back over to Austin's house to show him the videos of Din-Din. She felt a great need to find him and protect him from the world. First, she had to check and see if her cellphone was fully charged. She ran over to the phone to peek: "Yes! 100 percent!"

She grabbed it and the charging cord and grabbed a backpack and headed for the door.

While in flight Cho-Goon was very busy mapping, tracing, and retracing where the impact of the surge of power took place. Sweat beads on his forehead as he squints his eyes, focusing on terrain maps of this new foreign land. He knows that his life is at stake if he messes this up. The blast radius was so big for this particular event that there was no way he could miscalculate the coordinates. Just looking at the energy particles ranging from the ground all the way into the upper atmosphere of the planet and probably beyond, if it hit the radar of Lord Kull while on Planet Murn.

Cho-Goon began lowering the craft slowly to get to the ground zero location of whatever took place.

As the ship extended the legs to land, Lord Kull says: "Run a scan for potential life forms in the area, there will be destruction if we are met with another encounter!"

Cho-Goon: "Yes my lord!"

As the scan completes there are only miniature life forms that resemble small creatures. It is late at night in Earth time and the streets are quiet with no traffic.

Lord Kull: "Let's get to work!"

As the two exit the ship, Cho-Goon pulls out a small device and opens the palm of his hand and it takes off into the air. Once the drone like device reaches a certain position in the air, several different shades of light begin to emit. An entire scene starts to form of the fight that took place between Austin and Jimmy. The fight scene appears to be frozen at the point that Austin punches Jimmy. This device appears to be some modified version of a spectrophotometer. As the two move around studying the point of contact and reading the energy levels of the punch, Lord Kull can't believe the readings that he's getting.

Lord Kull: "This appears to be a being with great power that has created this energy signal."

Cho-Goon: "I have never seen readings like this before; the power seems to be coming from its hands!"

Lord Kull: "Cloak the ship! We must follow the traces of this being and find out once and for all what it is."

Cho-Goon races back to the ship to cloak it while it sits in an intersection.

Lord Kull begins to walk and follow the trail.

As Cho-Goon walks out of the ship he opens his hands with a motion and the drone like vehicle comes down and moves with him as he catches up with Lord Kull.

As they walk and the machine paints a picture of the beings and the energy surrounding them, Cho-Goon stops in his tracks when he notices a being that looks like the beings on the planet that they are actively invading.

Lord Kull: "Keep moving, we don't have time for sightseeing!"

Cho-Goon: "Yes my lord!"

After a few minutes of walking, they came to a group of tall buildings near each other. The two had made it to the alley behind Austin's building.

Knock knock knock

Austin heard the knock at the door and went to the hallway. He realized that his mother was asleep so he hurried to the door to answer. As he opened the door, he saw Brianna's face and let her in.

Brianna: "You gotta see this!" She pulls out her phone and begins showing Austin the videos that she saw earlier.

Austin: "This is crazy! So where do you think that he is now?"

Brianna: "I don't know, but we need to find him before somebody else does!"

Austin: "We gotta start somewhere and right now we have nowhere to start."

Tap tap tap tap

There was a light tapping coming from Austin's room window.

Austin and Brianna rushed to his room to see where the noise was coming from.

When they get there, they see Din-Din in front of the window. Brianna smiled ear to ear to see him outside the window and he smiled when he saw her as well. Austin rushed to open the window letting Din-Din inside.

Din-Din: "I have started preparing the ship and with a few slight adjustments we will be ready to make our trip to Murn and complete the mission!"

Austin: "What mission?"

Din-Din: "The mission of freeing my people and destroying the evil monster that..."

Austin: "What?!"

Din-Din: "Come with me to the top of your structure."

All three of them go out to the hallway and take the stairs up to the roof.

It took a few minutes for Austin to break the emergency exit for the roof but when the door opened Austin and Brianna stood with their mouths opened wide in awe at the sight in front of them.

Din-Din: "This is how we will get back to my home planet and save them!"

Austin and Brianna slowly walk out towards the ship in disbelief and wonder, making sure not to get too close to the unknown object in front of them.

Brianna: "It's a real spaceship! I can't believe that it's a real spaceship!" (pulling out her phone to take pictures)

Austin: "Wow Din-Din, this is Amazing!"

Din-Din: "Just a few minor repairs and we should be ready to..."

At that moment his hair stood straight up and you could sense fear in his body language.

Brianna: "Din-Din what's wrong?!"

Din-Din: "He's Here!"

Quintan Bizzell

The Stand-Off

Din-Din rushes to the edge of the rooftop to veer over the ledge. The kids follow him to take a look but what they saw sparked a lot of questions.

Austin: "What is that big thing?!"

Brianna: "Yeah and what is the little thing next to it?!"

While the kids were talking, Din-Din started running towards the staircase headed downstairs.

Brianna: "Oh, he's pissed!" (while running behind)

Austin: "Stop him before he gets hurt!" (While running behind Brianna)

The three go flying down the stairs at top speed, but Din-Din had about a 15 ft head start, and he didn't appear to be slowing down. As they hit the last flight Din-Din had already busted the door open and bolted outside. Both teens, hands on their knees leaning over breathing.

Brianna: "Man I didn't know he was that fast!"

Austin: "We gotta catch up with him, come on!" (grabbing Brianna and taking off)

As they approached, Din-Din had stopped in front of a very large creature that looked like a lizard and a fairly normal sized creature with the face of a pig.

Brianna: "Whoaaaa!"

Austin approaches Din-Din and puts his right hand on his shoulder, Din-Din pushes his hand away and begins to speak.

Din-Din: "Where are my parents!? And what have you done to our elders?!"

Lord Kull: "Punish him, then tie all of them up. We shall take them with us. The Master will be pleased once he sees what we have captured!"

Cho-Goon: "I saw this one on the energy readings where we landed."

Brianna: (eyes wide open as if she's terrified) "They want to capture us?!"

Austin: "Chill, Bri nobody's getting captured here."

Din-Din charges towards the creatures.

Lord Kull steps back and Cho-Goon unholsters a strange whip and steps up.

As Din-Din jumps to swing a punch, he is met with a boot to the chest that knocks the wind out of him and leaves him on the ground in a cloud of dust.

Cho-Goon then swings the whip and when it makes contact with Din-Din, it begins to shock him, leaving him shaking and making a gurgling sound.

Brianna screams and starts to cry while going over to help him. Lord Kull lets out a monstrously deep laugh at the sight of Din-Din shaking and gurgling.

Cho-Goon moves forward to do more damage, only to be met by Austin.

Austin puts his hand out to tell Cho-Goon to stop and Cho-Goon swung the whip. Austin caught the whip with his left hand and imagined himself absorbing the electricity to become stronger. When he noticed that it worked, he snatched the whip and yanked Cho-Goon to him and landed a right-handed punch that rocked Cho-Goon.

Austin then wrapped the whip tighter around his left hand and hit him again while he was dazed. The second hit landed in the middle of Cho-Goon's back, making him squeal and sending him flying into Lord Kull.

Lord Kull catches Cho-Goon, grabs him by the face and pushes him back towards Austin and says: "Stop wasting time and finish this creature!"

During the fight, Lord Kull is seen measuring the power levels of Austin, using his special reader that covered his left eye. Brianna noticed that while watching him like a hawk. She took notice once she saw it light up several times during the fight and wondered what the device was for.

The last punch thrown by Austin forced Cho-Goon to let go of the whip. Austin tossed the whip to the side and stood his ground waiting to see what Cho-Goon was going to try next. Cho-Goon looked uneasy coming back to the fight, almost as if he was afraid of Austin.

Austin took notice of this and says: "This can all be over if you just tell me where my friend's parents are"

Cho-Goon- "They're all our slaves now and once I'm done with you, you'll join them."

Austin clenched his fist and Cho-Goon charged towards him. As Cho-Goon picked up speed and got closer he put his head down and rammed Austin, carrying him backwards all the way into the side of some dumpsters.

As Cho-Goon backed off you can hear the sinister laughter of Lord Kull in the background. While recovering from the impact of the hit, Austin heard a ringing in his right ear. At that same time Din-Din was waking up in Brianna's Arms.

Brianna: "Those creatures are trying to make us their slaves and they're hurting Austin!"

Din-Din: "Does he believe?" (while shaking off the grogginess from waking up)

Brianna: "Does he believe what, that we're about to be alien food! oh shhh-...." (she jumps up and yells to Austin) "They're going to eat us!"

Austin's eyes widen with fear.

Austin: "Wait what? They're going to do what!"

Brianna looks at Din-Din and says: "I think he believes now!" Austin gets up with an angry look on his face.

Brianna: "The big mean one is looking up recipes on how to cook us!"

The energy reader goes from the hundreds to the point of blinking and showing zeros. You can see Lord Kull tapping the eyewear to try to fix the error.

Brianna: "I think he's found the recipe Austin!"

Cho-Goon rushes Austin for another charge attack. This time Austin was ready, he takes one step back and delivers a right-handed punch aimed at the head of Cho-Goon. In slow motion you could see dust and dirt particles lifting off of the ground and moving with the motion of his punch. As he connected the punch to Cho-Goon's forehead in a downward motion, another flash of light was produced causing all of the windows on the first-floor apartments and car windows to shatter in the vicinity. The force from the punch sent Cho-Goon chin first into the ground and sent him flying backwards creating a trench in the old blacktop.

The noise from the back alley and the flash had started to draw a crowd. People began coming out of the back of the building to see what they believed to be an altercation. When you look up you could see people in their windows, people opening windows some yelling for the noise to stop and others just watching.

Breathing heavily while staring at what he just did, Austin heard lots of chatter coming from behind him. Lord Kull could not believe his energy reader and what he just witnessed; he sprang forth with tremendous speed.

Austin, had his back turned looking at the crowd that had formed. He saw the people start running away in fear as he was picked up from behind and thrown backwards. He covered his head and face as he smashed into the side of a dumpster. To his surprise the impact didn't hurt. Austin stood up to realize that he had been thrown completely across the alley, and when he looked at where he landed there was a massive dent in the side of the dumpster. He looked at his hands and tightened his fists, he felt his strength growing.

Lord Kull: "I am Lord Kull! (With his hands raised) I have never seen a creature such as yourself, your strength, your speed, what are you? I've conquered many planets but I have not come across anything with such power. What is your secret?"

Austin: "You wanna know my secret? I was given a gift and the friend that gave me this gift asked that in return I help him save his family! (As Austin starts moving towards Lord Kull with his fists clenched) He said that you have taken his family, is this true!?"

He stops just feet away from the giant creature. Taking in the size and all of the features of the monstrous being in front of him.

Austins mother was in the kitchen getting a glass of water and peeked out of the kitchen window and noticed a crowd. When she saw that her son was outside and at the center of everyone's attention, she grabbed her jacket and hurried out to the hallway to the stairs.

Lord Kull: "The only choice that you have is to join me. I have a use for your power. Stand by my side, if you refuse, I will destroy you and enslave this pathetic planet. (as he points to all of the people in the area) Take a knee and devote your lives to Master On....."

Austin interrupts him and says: "Maybe all those muscles are covering your ears and you didn't hear me so I'll ask again!"

Lord Kull lunges forward with a punch. Austin turns his head away from the punch while grabbing the arm and hip tossing the giant onto the ground leaving him sliding a few feet.

Lord Kull being slammed onto the pavement caused the ground to shake. Lord Kull landed near Brianna and Din-Din, as he got up Brianna shouted: "I bet you can hear him now huh!"

Lord Kull grabbed the nearest dumpster with two hands and hurled it at Brianna, Just missing her and hitting a few onlookers behind her.

After the narrow escape she ran to get behind Austin. Lord Kull grabs another dumpster and launches it at Austin, and charges. As Austin knocks the dumpster the away, he is met with both fists sending him violently rolling on the ground. This was by far the hardest Austin has ever been hit, he held his chest in pain from the hit as he laid on the ground. As he stood up to face Lord Kull, a brick flies over and hits Lord Kull on the side of his head and a lady's voice came from the crowd.

Bonnie: "Leave my son alone!" As she steps forward and directly into the path of the monster.

Austin: "Mom! Wait no...."

Lord Kull: "Is that so...." (While rubbing his hands together)

As Lord Kull moves to grab Bonnie he is smashed into and rammed into the side of a car in the back parking lot.

Lord Kull stood up and rushed Austin with a barrage of punches that Austin could not stop. As he took every punishing punch, he tried to envision the punches slowing down so that he could catch one, it started to work! He grabbed Lord Kull's right hand and as soon as he had it, Lord Kull grabbed hold of him with the other hand, let out a blood curdling scream like a dinosaur and threw him up through the third-floor brick wall of Austin's building. The impact of the brick wall immediately knocked Austin out.

Brianna: "Noooo noooo nooooo! It's not supposed to end like this!"

Police sirens start sounding off and for some reason that really aggravated Lord Kull. He saw the cop car approaching and grabbed a vehicle from the lot and launched it into the moving police car, crushing the front end and silencing the police siren. He turned to where he threw Austin and started walking to the building.

Bonnie went over to Brianna who was crying with her head down and comforted her. Din-Din closed his eyes and tried to reach Austin telepathically. He kept getting nothing but darkness. After his 3rd attempt Austin woke up. He showed Austin a glimpse of his mother and sister crying. He said to Austin (They believe in you! Do you believe?)

Austin sat up and gasped for air as if he had been holding his breath.

Lord Kull jumped up and began to climb into the hole that he threw Austin into. He climbed in and stood up and was met by a devastating punch!

A light so bright flashed from the hole in the building and Lord Kull was seen flying backwards out of the hole and down to the parking lot with Austin right behind him in the air. As Lord Kull landed onto the ground Austin landed on top of him hammering both of his fists into Lord Kull's chest! The crowd erupted with cheer. Austin began hitting Lord Kull one punch at a time, left then right repeatedly, and on the final right punch, Lord Kull's energy reader flew off of his head and onto the ground.

Brianna broke free of Bonnie's hold and ran over, grabbed the energy reader and ran into a nearby crowd. Shaking from the adrenaline she put the reader onto her head; it started to move while making a mechanical noise and clicked into place. Lots of symbols and numbers started to flash in front of her right eye and then she heard a voice, a female voice. The voice was so low that she couldn't really hear what it was saying.

Appearing to be out cold Lord Kull laid there lifeless. As Austin climbs off of him, he locks eyes with Cho-Goon, who stood there in amazement because he has never seen anyone stop Lord Kull let alone disagree with him. As his eyes rapidly went from Lord Kull and to Austin back and forth, Austin could tell that he no longer wanted to fight. Austin walks over to his mother.

Austin: "It's ok, Mom, I'm ok!"

She rushes over and hugs him tightly. Just as she hugs him several screams came from where he left Lord Kull. As he looked over, Lord Kull was gone.

Din-Din: "He has my family; we have to save them!"

Austin: "How?"

Din-Din: "We must catch him, It's time! We must get to the ship!" (he starts running towards the building) Brianna follows him.

Austin looks at his mother and says: "I will be back soon; I have to help my friend." (And he takes off behind them to the building.)

In the air hovering over the scene, a news helicopter is seen with a reporter hanging out of the side with a camera man and a microphone talking into the camera.

Reporter: "After a gruesome fight the young teenager has saved Earth from an alien invasion, wait on the roof! It appears that the teenager is boarding a spacecraft!"

As Austin follows Brianna into the ship, they see Cho-Goon standing at the door to the ship. Brianna: "He's trying to stop us!"

Cho-Goon: "No, I am here to serve my new master!" (Everyone looks at Austin)

Brianna: "Master?!"

Austin: "Get in, we could use some help, where is Lord Kull's ship?"

Cho-Goon: "It's over there!"

As the ship lifts off and moves into the direction of Lord Kull, they see the ship accelerating from the street into the night sky.

Brianna: "Where is he going?"

Cho-Goon: "Back to your friend's planet for reinforcements, we must get there first and stop him!"

Din-Din: "I am setting the course, hold on!"

Brianna: "To whaaa!"

The ship takes off so fast that everyone inside the ship started moving in slow motion and the stars that were in the sky looked like streaks of light passing by. All of a sudden, the ship stopped and all of the power went out.

Din-Din: "No not again!"

Austin: "Again?"

Brianna: "What do you mean not ag....ohhhhhhhhhh shhhh!"

The ship began falling backwards towards Earth's upper atmosphere. Austin and Brianna started screaming. Cho-Goon started scrambling around until he opened the floor of the ship. As he climbed inside you could see that he was looking for something. In a few seconds the ship powered on and blasted forward once again. Shaken by the drop, both Brianna and Austin immediately began vomiting where they were standing.

Cho-Goon rushes up, closes the floor panel and hurries to the only other seat next to Din-Din and starts touching buttons.

Din-Din: "How do you know how to operate our ancient technology?"

Cho-Goon: "Although it is ancient and out of date, this craft is built like any other lower class light cruiser in every galaxy I have visited."

Din-Din: "This is state of the art, top of the line sacred....."

Cho-Goon: "Yeah yeah! This is space rubbish!"

Din-Din lunges towards Cho-Goon choking him with both hands down to the floor of the craft. As the two wrestle,

Austin snaps out of his ill daze and says: "Enough! He's trying to help save your family let him go!"

The two stop, get up and get back into their seats and get back to navigating the craft.

Austin: "How long does it take to get to...." (Austin collapses to the floor and is out cold)

Upon him collapsing he woke up immediately and found himself standing in a different location. It felt like a room, the room was warm and it was very foggy. He couldn't make out anything in the room. It was like a spotlight was on him and the rest of the area around him was foggy. What was strange to Austin is that he couldn't move any part of his body but his eyes. He saw a shadow move swiftly from left to right in front of him causing his heart rate to go up and made him nervous. A voice sounded as if it was inside of his head asked

Voice: "Whoooooo are you?"

Austin: "My name is Austin"

Voice: "Well Austin, it's a pleasure to meet you."

Austin: "Who are you, and why can't I see you?"

Voice: "My name is Oridio On'doon, throughout many galaxies I'm known as Master On'doon."

Austin: "Many galaxies? If you're a master then why do you hide? Why not come out and…"

Right in front of Austin's view what looked like a hooded person was starting to form. Austin couldn't really make out what the person looks like, just a hooded person hiding their face with a long skinny nose like a witch of some sort.

Austin: "How did you do that, and why can't I move?"

Master On'Doon: "I can do many things. You can't move because you're not really here!"

Austin: "What do you mean?"

Master On'Doon: "I'm not really here either, we're both inside your mind."

Master On'Doon begins to move slowly around Austin, poking at him with his skinny finger, he began measuring his height and squeezing his arms and legs. This angered Austin because he couldn't stop him.

Austin: "Why are you doing this"

On'Doon: "I'm going to add you to my collection"

Austin got so angry that he snapped his hand loose and swung at the hooded figure, knocking him down to the ground. At that very moment Austin woke up and sat up and realized that he was back on the ships floor with everyone around him.

Brianna: "Are you ok?"

Austin: "I guess."

Brianna: "Din-Din help him off the floor."

Austin: "I'm alright. I don't need any help."

Brianna: "Not you, him!"

As Austin looks over, he sees Cho-Goon upside down up against the wall of the ship.

Brianna: "I don't know what you were dreaming about but he heard you and tried to wake you up and let's just say we will all let you sleep next time."

Austin: "ahhhhhhhhhhh"

As a wave of pain pulsed through his head, it dropped him to his knees. Brianna helps him up.

Austin: "I don't think I like being in space! How long until we get to your home Din-Din?"

Din-Din: "We have about 184,000 kilometers"

Austin: "What does that.."

Cho-Goon: "We are slowly approaching the speed needed to jump to hyperspace, this will shorten the distance to minutes my Lord!"

Austin: "See Din-Din, that's how you should explain things, take notes."

Brianna: "We have about 100,000,000 metronautical nauts hahahaaa" (making fun of Din-Din)

Cho-Goon: "Beating him back to the planet should not be difficult, he only has one small fuel cell left to make it back. That's if he didn't burn through it already."

Austin: "Well we need to get there fast and develop a plan before he gets there"

Din-Din: "I'm ready!"

Cho-Goon: "We are now in the window to make the jump to warp my Lord, on your command"

Brianna: "My Lord on your command" (quietly while giggling)

Austin smiles and says: "Stop it! And what's that thing on your eye?"

Brianna: "It's my special power space thingy" (smacking Austin's hand as he reaches to touch it)

Austin: "Well what does it do?"

Brianna: "I'm still trying to figure it out"

Cho-Goon: "My Lord"

Austin: "Right, hit it!"

Cho -Goon: "Secure your positions!"

Brianna: "What does that even me.."

The ship immediately disappeared

Lord Kull: "Andona!" (He's seen screaming into the communication device. He's battered and covered in dirt and debris)

"Andona" he screams again.

Master On'doon: "Now that you have decided to go against my orders, I have shut down your ability to give orders. What have you been up to? Planning to over throw me? Taking my ships and my soldiers to do your own bidding!"

Lord Kull: "Master, I would never disobey you! I wanted to give you a great gift!"

Master On'Doon: "Ahhhhh yes, the gift that almost killed you and left you running and flailing back home in fear like a frightened little waxlian!"

Lord Kull: "Master, I beg you, please allow me to continue the mission to completion. I have a plan, and this time there will be no one to stop me!"

(All of a sudden Lord Kull begins to scream and cover his ears almost as if some kind of sound was causing him pain)

Master On'Doon: "This is your last chance to disappoint me!"

(Lord Kull screams louder from the pressure in his head intensifying)

Master On'Doon: "Your head will explode if you fail this time! Finish the job, and do it in a reasonable time, or I will destroy you, recreate you and destroy you again!"

Lord Kull: "Yes master!"

The communication device clicks and a bit of green liquid drips from Lord Kull's nostril opening.

Meanwhile on Planet Murn

Soldier 1: "This area has been thoroughly exhausted of all resources, begin prep for location three. Separate the females from the males and once separated, start the onboarding process, Master On'Doon's orders!"

The rest of the soldiers remove their hands from the saluting position and all stomp at the same time and get moving to do their jobs. In that area there was at least five hundred Wachooti people working, including Din-Din's mother, father and little brother.

They were all completely drained, their clothes torn and they all looked like they haven't had any food or water for quite some time.

This type of work was not an everyday thing on their home world, the Wachooti people believed in living alongside nature and in harmony.

As the soldiers got closer to Din-Din's family, they kept shifting to the back of the crowd to avoid being separated but eventually a soldier reached out for his mother's hand and was met with a push from Din-Din's father. His young brother started to scream and cry as several soldiers surrounded his father and mother. The father gripped his wife's hand tight and refused to let it go. One of the soldiers whipped a baton like weapon out and it extended to the point of hearing it snap into place. The son ran over towards the father and was grabbed by his collar and taken away, the father motioned towards his screaming child and was struck with the baton across the back repeatedly and electrocuted with every blow until he weakened. As his mother sobbed, they drug her away and took the father and son to be with the rest of the males in shackles.

The Order of On'Doon specialize in the complete destruction of the planets that they choose to occupy. This process happens in steps. The first step is to locate all resources and map them. Next, they begin mining all of the resources that were mapped out one location at a time. While these processes are happening there is a science department that is tasked with collecting and logging information about every species of animal and plant life on the planet before the planet becomes unstable and too environmentally volatile to conduct research. The last step in most cases is to round up the captured inhabitants and load them onto ships and use them as infantry to repeat the same process on other planets until they expire.

Meanwhile the females of every species are to be studied and more than likely used for some sort of genetic cross breeding experiments.

sound of power going out

Din-Din began trying to find the source of the power outage with Cho-Goon. As they both went to the opening in the floor of the ship, Din-Din stops and stands still with tears in his eyes.

Brianna: "Hey, What's wrong?"

Din-Din: "Someone's hurting my family and I can't get to them and save them"

Austin: "Who's hurting your family?"

Din-Din: "I don't know but I can feel my mother's pain"

Power comes back on

Cho-Goon emerges from the opening.

Cho-Goon: "This giant galactic piece of (as he looks at Din-Din he changes this face to a smile) wonder and history, always full of surprises, shall we!"

The two go back to the seats

Din-Din: "We have to reenter all information and…."

Cho-Goon: "The planet is close enough to get there swiftly without warp, let's not risk another power failure plus the health of our passengers."

Brianna: "Make it so!"

Austin: "Ok Star Trek! Yeah, let's do that, but let's get there fast, we're already late to the party!"

Din-Din: "The party?"

Austin: "Yeah it's like, never mind, let's hurry up!"

Cho-Goon: "Brace yourselves!" (As he lets out a small snort)

As the ship speeds up Austin is seen looking at Din-Din as if he is worried about him. Din-Din seems to be losing hope for his family and his body language shows it. He was down, this made Austin upset.

Brianna: "Wow, is that where we're going!?"

Din-Din lifted his head up and his eyes widened with joy.

Din-Din: "I never thought that I would make it back."

Cho-Goon: "just a few more kilometers and we can begin the landing sequences."

As both of the teenager's stare at the planet becoming bigger and bigger, each minute you could tell that they had all sorts of thoughts running through their imagination about what to expect, after all this was their first time leaving Earth.

Cho-Goon: "Brace yourselves for some light turbulence"

The ship starts to rock back and forth violently for about 3 minutes. It was so strong that Austin felt like the ship was gonna crash. All of a sudden, the movement calmed down.

Austin: "You said that it would be light turbulence!"

Cho-Goon: "It was the best that we could do given that this is an (looks over at Din-Din while talking with a smile) aged and finely preserved vessel from long ago Master"

Brianna: "Bro you really gotta chill with the master after every sentence, it's kinda weird!"

Austin: "Don't mind her Cho-Goon, carry-on." (he moves his hand in a carry-on gesture)

As the ship begins to slow down and lower itself, the two teenagers were glued to the window of the ship.

Brianna: "Look, they have trees!"

Din-Din: "Yes we have trees just like your planet"

Where they decided to put the ship down wasn't close to Din-Din's home, instead it was on the outskirts in a far more wooded area where no one would notice them landing.

Cho-Goon: "This is where we will land!"

Austin: "How do you know that it's safe?"

Cho-Goon: "I know the exact coordinates of where we began our raid of this planet, I picked the location"

Din-Din stands up and Austin shoves him back down with one hand on his right shoulder.

Austin: "That was in the past, he's changed now Din-Din, he's going to help us save your family." (An alarm goes off)

Cho-Goon: "Master, I have initiated the landing sequence"

Din-Din looks over at Cho-Goon acknowledging that he is quite the pilot with a nod and a half smile. As the door lifts up and a landing ramp deploys, the two teens stand in the doorway waiting to get the ok to step out onto the new strange planet.

Brianna: "Look Austin, it's just like Earth, without the buildings!"

Austin: "Or the smog, it smells like fresh cut grass!"

The

Resistance

Din-Din: "Let's move!"

Everyone follows Din-Din down the ramp and into a swamp like area.

Din-Din: "We are not far from the city, try not to get wet, the wheedles are horrible this time of day and if you get wet and you're warm they will feed on you."

Austin: "Feed on us!?"

Din-Din: "Yes they bite and leave bumps that make you scratch yourself."

Brianna: "Oh like mosquitoes."

Austin: "Yeah, like mosquitoes!"

As they drudge on through the marshy landscape the teens notice that there are lots of what appear to be birds flying by very quickly.

Brianna: "There are birds everywhere!"

Austin: "Yeah they're flying pretty close to my head too, is that normal here?"

Brianna: "Ummmm" (Standing still with a bug-like creature that resembled a hummingbird with a very long, needle like sharp beak hovering in front of her face)

Austin: "Umm whaaa (While turning around) Brianna don't move!"

Din-Din: "Come to me"

Brianna starts to move towards Din-Din. Din-Din's eyes change in color and the insect becomes locked on Din-Din's gaze. Then out of nowhere it darts off.

Brianna: "Hey what did you just do!?"

Din-Din: "Showed it a group of paragoggins bathing at the water's edge, wheedles are easily distracted with food. Let's go!"

He starts moving quickly during the trek to get to the destination.

It seems that Cho-Goon is very observant and only speaks if he has valuable knowledge that can help. Maybe the years of getting beaten for speaking out without being asked has made him the type to not have unwarranted outbursts or speak so freely for fear of the consequences. So, he follows the group and stays in his own head for the most part. At the same time, he's also new to the environment on this new planet, after all he was only here for a short period of time during the invasion. He wasn't really used to discovering new lands without violence being involved so he wasn't used to this type of exploration.

On planet Murn the wind blows down creating quite a different from Earth look. For instance, most of the larger trees are shaped like mushrooms because of the airflow to the environment. One tree in particular that is the sacred tree of the Wachooti people, the Aboondalla tree, is a very large tree with a weatherproof canopy that makes them very popular to live under on planet Murn. Most of the Wachooti people live within these trees. These trees are gifts from the Wachooti elders during wedding ceremonies whenever a family is formed. The family is connected to the tree spiritually during the ceremony and is forever bonded with the tree. They are never to cut the tree or damage it in any way; it is a part of their family like a living being because it is.

As the family grows it grows with them. It is said that the elders know when there is an ailment within the family by looking at the condition of the Aboondalla trees leaves. That's how they know to bring prayer and counsel to families in need, not everyone is open to discussing illnesses within their families. The area that the group is headed to is like grand central station for Aboondalla trees all circling one humongous tree. It is the grand Aboondalla tree and its roots are believed to be wrapped around the heart of their small planet. Legend has it that the planet whispers to the elders through the branches under the canopy.

Austin: "Man I don't know what it is but I feel great!"

Brianna: "Why are you so loud, we are supposed to be sneaking, you know creeping up?"

Austin: "I know, but it's like I can feel my blood pulsating through my veins right now and it feels like a rush of energy."

Din-Din stops and examines Austin for a moment, internally asking himself: "Could it be the large Wachootium deposits underground causing the young hero to feel this way?" Then he shakes his head and goes back to walking the trail.

Din-Din: "We are getting close to the outer villages where I live, so we must stay focused, my family could be anywhere"

In this area there are lots of older looking makeshift fences around the Aboondalla trees. The group hustled past what looked like an area with stores set up under the Aboondalla trees, with merchandise hanging from the branches.

Din-Din heard noises up ahead of the group coming from a large tree that had objects in the yard area that resembled things that children would play with. As they got closer the noise got louder. They observed a group of about eight of what appeared to be lizards in skin tight black body suits with helmets. They were not very large but they had tails and they were communicating with a loud clicking sound. Around their waist you could see a belt with a baton or a club looking object. The lizard group seemed to be approaching the large tree and calling out to the inhabitants in the tree. There was one adult protecting multiple small Wachooti children.

Din-Din: "We must stop them; the little ones need us."

The lizard group rushed the tree and grabbed the adult and hit it with a club and this sent an electric shock causing the adult Wachooti to scream, it sounded like a females scream. (After a few hits Brianna could no longer take it and came out from her hiding place)

The lizard group had grabbed several of the smaller Wachooti and you could hear them whimpering. They were trying to hold each other's hands to keep from being taken. Brianna took off running across to the yard, breezing past the first few soldiers and pushes one that appears to be struggling to separate two of the children.

Brianna: "Let them go!"

Austin and the rest of the group follow. The soldiers are now aware that they have company and turn to face them.

Cho-Goon approaches them and his voice changes to a series of clicks.

Cho-Goon: "Stand down and release the prisoners"

Soldier # 1: "We no longer take orders from anyone but the one true Massssssssster!" (As he pulls his baton and strikes Cho-Goon in the shoulder)

The other four soldiers advance and two of them grab and start beating Cho-Goon. Brianna is seen in a tug of war with one of the lizard soldiers over a small Wachooti child when Austin runs up and kicks another soldier into the soldier that she was struggling with causing him to release the small Wachooti child. The sudden release of the child sent Brianna and the child backwards causing Brianna to hit the back of her head on the large tree.

At the moment of impact, the accessory that she had stolen from Lord Kull and attached to her head pierced through her skin like a needle and sent a sharp pain like the worst headache ever along with a loud ringing noise through her skull.

As she laid there on the ground with a tear running down her cheek, numbers and weird symbols started to appear flashing quickly on the screen of the eyewear. All that she could do was lay there because the noise was so strong along with the pain that it was paralyzing. In the distance you can see Austin battling with two soldiers and an additional soldier backs away and touches what looks to be a button on an earpiece and lets out a weird noise and runs away. The other soldiers begin to collect themselves and back away slowly.

Cho-Goon gets up with dirt all over and a few scratches on his face and says: "They just called for reinforcements; we should find somewhere to hide!"

Austin: "I didn't fly all the way over here to hide, get the little ones and take them to the safest place that you know of Din-Din, I'm Going to do what I promised you that I would do!" (as he looks at Din-Din with a smile)

Cho-Goon: "Then I shall stand with you and withstand whatever punishment or victory that comes" (as he limps towards Austin)

There was something strange happening with Austin, it was an extreme confidence building up. He felt stronger, and during the last fight he felt unbothered almost in a euphoric state, as if his fear had washed away and he now truly believes that he is powerful. The only place that Din-Din could think of that was an unknown safe place was the harmonic defense system. No one ever went there except for he and a few elders.

Din-Din: "Ok, ok, it's ok now. (hushing the frightened young Wachooti) Let's all grab a toy and get in line, we're going on an adventure." (with a smile on his face)

He was thinking of a route that would lead past his little tool shed so that he could grab some tools to help him attempt to repair the hds.

185

Out of nowhere the Wachooti teacher says;

Ms. Pincey: "That's right children, let's all get in line and keep our hands to ourselves and remember, the ancestors are watching. (with a smile) (all of the children say the phrase along with the teacher) Alright let's go my loves! She walks over to Din-Din and gives him a huge hug and says: "You have saved us, I'm so proud of what you have become! The ancestors will surely bless you and I know that your parents are proud."

Din-Din: "Thank you, do you know where I can find my parents?"

Ms. Pincey: "When they started putting our people in chains, I took the children and came back here and we have been held up ever since. The children need food and water."

Din-Din: "Ok, let's go."

As they start down the trail Austin says: "We will find your parents and they will be safe."

Din-Din nods his head, turns back around and disappears into the brush with the teacher and the children.

Brianna, while still on the ground starts to sit up. The noise has stopped but she hears a female voice that sounds far away like a telephone call but the volume was very low.

Brianna: "Hello?"

Voice: "Hello."

Brianna: "Hey, who is this?"

Voice: "Hey, who is this?"

Brianna: "Why do you keep saying whatever I.."

She felt a vibration on the right side of her head and heard the voice get louder. It sounded just like her.

Voice: "Neural connection established, human, female, Earth, English, heads up display initiated."

The accessory started to target things in Brianna's vision like trees and the distances between her and objects. It was like an information overload.

Brianna: "Hey! Wait a minute what are you?"

Voice: "I'm whatever you want me to be, but right now I'm you, or an extension of you. I'm here to assist you."

Brianna: "So, what do we do now?"

Voice: "Just sit tight while I continue to run diagnostics and gather more data about our surroundings. Actually, you can't sit tight, there is a young human with an unreadable power level advancing."

Brianna: "Hey! Wait, can you play music, you gotta be able to play...."

Austin: "Who are you talking to?"

Brianna: "I was just singing a song."

Austin: "So you picked now out of all times to sing a song?"

Brianna: "Yeah brotha, in trying times people sing songs to boost morale!"

Austin: "I know that this experience is far out and pretty weird, I just want to make sure that you're ok."

Brianna: "Honestly, I kinda miss home and I know my mother is worried sick about me."

Austin approaches Brianna and gives her a hug and says: "I miss home too; it's time to finish the job so that we can get back. I'm going to need your help though, are you ready?"

Brianna nods her head

Austin: "Ok, then let's do this! Where would they have retreated to?"

Cho-Goon: "There has to be a small camp nearby where they can..."

Brianna while walking says: "Hey look I can see some ships from here!"

Cho-Goon: "We must be close to ground zero."

Austin: "Hey, I can't see anything, how can you see the ships?"

Brianna not realizing that nothing was visible due to all of the large trees almost blocking the entire view says: "I see three large ships, one larger than the other two, approximately 2.6 kilometers north of us, you guys are blind!"

Austin's mouth was wide open as he listened to Brianna.

Austin: "Wow!"

Brianna: "But at the pace that we're moving it will take twenty-four minutes fifty-three seconds to reach the ships."

Austin: "Wait how do…"

Brianna: "Shhhhh!" She motions for everyone to stop.

The sound of multiple people's footsteps starts to get louder.

Brianna: "14,14,17, oh that one says 27…"

Austin: "What are you talking about?"

Brianna: "You asked for my help, I'm just telling you what I see."

Austin: (Whispers) "Yeah but when did you start seeing numbers?"

The footsteps stop and a series of clicks start.

Cho-Goon: "They know something is up."

Austin: "Let them take me and follow us. It will lead us to Din-Din's family, trust me."

Brianna: "I don't like this idea."

Cho-Goon: "It is a brilliant idea, Master!"

Austin: (Whispers) "Hide, get down!"

Austin steps out and begins running away from the footsteps and the group begins to chase him. Just as they get closer, Austin slows down and puts his hands up. The biggest soldier strikes Austin across the back with a club and electrocutes him and he falls to the ground. Brianna stands up and Cho-Goon pulls her back down into the bushes as they watch Austin get hit repeatedly by the soldiers as they drag him off. As the soldiers drag Austin away Cho-Goon says: "Once they get far enough, we will begin to follow."

Brianna: "Ok"

Din-Din: "Once we get to the edge of town, take the children up the hill to the monument, it is the safest place for them right now. I will grab some tools and meet you there shortly."

Ms. Pincey: "But what if you get caught?"

Din-Din: "I will be swift; I only need a few things, hurry and take them."

Din-Din races off at the sight of the edge of town towards his small makeshift lab. As he gets closer to his shack he smells smoke. He gets to the door of his lab and bolts inside. While rummaging through his tools he hears the sound of several footsteps, almost like people marching. He stops moving and peeks out of the corner of the window. He sees several soldiers marching while surrounding someone, they're at a distance though so he couldn't see who the prisoner was so he looks on and waits for them to get closer.

Austin: "Where are you taking me?" (The lizard-like men don't respond and continue dragging Austin)

Austin: "I said, where are you..."

Austin was met with a very hard blow to the back that stunned him for a moment. Austin was very angry but had to hold it in, he didn't want to spoil the plan. The soldier that hit him screamed in Austin's face and all that Austin could think about was the horrific smell that came out of its mouth. As the group marched on, they marched by the window that Din-Din was looking out of. Din-Din's heart rate skyrocketed when he saw that it was Austin that was the prisoner. He began thinking that it was over and that there was no way that they could save his planet. He didn't know what to do. Out of nowhere he felt that it was his duty to fight the monsters and free Austin. He grabbed a long pipe that was left lying around and stepped outside.

Din-Din: "Let my friend go, now!"

(As he slapped the pole on his left palm)

Austin looked up to see that it was Din-Din, he yelled: "Din-Din, nooo, run!"

(Everyone stopped walking and turned around)

There was a low clicking noise from the larger soldier and three of the other soldiers started to advance towards Din-Din. Before they got close, Din-Din picked up a medium sized rock and threw it at the first soldier then disappeared. The soldiers stopped and looked confused for a second, then the first soldier got hit very hard in the head with the pipe and fell. The other soldiers started to look around. The second soldier got hit in the leg and let out a noise. As Din-Din moved around with the pipe he was invisible but the pipe wasn't, the larger soldier noticed this and made a clicking sound and two soldiers ran up and tackled Din-Din to the ground. Brianna went to move toward the soldiers and once again Cho-Goon had to grab her and pull her back. The soldiers picked Din-Din up and started to beat him from all angles until his body went limp from the punishment, there was no more fight left. Brianna cried silent tears in the bushes nearby and Cho-Goon looked on as the soldiers began to move forward with their new prisoners. The walk behind the soldiers seemed like forever but a small city of giant tree homes decorated with paints and gardens, some even had ropes to swing from.

As they got farther in, the view of the three massive ships got closer and closer. Austin watched as they passed by cages of Wachooti prisoners, looking as if they're about to be hauled off. The cages, filled with what looked to be mostly female and children of the Wachooti, judging by their appearances, had wheels, and the cages were made from wood. As Brianna and Cho-Goon were slowly sneaking behind them they began breaking open the latches and letting the Wachooti people free and signaling for them to be quiet. The walking came to a halt and the two soldiers who had Austin by the arms began taking him to another group of soldiers that looked to have a huge group of Wachooti people digging inside of a giant crater.

Several of them were walking around the perimeter as if they were on watch. After reaching the town, Brianna and Cho-Goon could not follow Austin and Din-Din anymore due to there being no more cover for them to hide, so they had to watch from a distance.

Cho-Goon: "What do you see little one?"

Brianna: "Ummmm, ok wait, there's lots of numbers here so give me a second. There are about seventeen soldier guys with small numbers, none over fourteen. And I see like seven larger soldier dudes with over twenty, and something huge just, wait never mind, it disappeared." Cho-Goon: "Good, it sounds like you're adjusting to your new neurological enhancement."

Brianna: "Wait, so you know?"

Cho -Goon: "Yes, now tell me how far away they are and what will be the best approach to eliminating them all."

Brianna: "Well, it says that they are one hundred and forty yards..." (voice corrects Brianna)

Voice: "Approximately 148.6 yards away."

Brianna: "I mean 148.6 yards away, and getting into the biggest ship that is 310 yards northeast of here and pushing the red button to the left will eliminate all life on this planet including us if we can't escape."

Cho -Goon: "A glorious victory indeed, but we mustn't vaporize the entire planet! What's the alternative?"

Brianna: "The next suggested course of action would be an attack using blunt force with sturdy objects that inflict enough damage to stop the threat."

Cho-Goon scans the area looking for weapons and notices large wagons filled with rocks from the mining excavation.

Cho-Goon: "That's it! The stones, we throw the stones, let's go!"

The two start moving quickly towards the area around the rocks that have been put into makeshift wagons and pulled away from the mining site.

The two soldiers holding Austin by the arms begin pushing his head down towards the ground as a huge lizard-like soldier walks over with some sort of neck collar. Din-Din begins to wake up and look around at his surroundings. He seems lost for a moment until he locks eyes with his mother while scanning the crowd of females that were lined up in a group waiting to be moved to a different location. He screams: "Mom!"

Austin's ears perked up and he looks around and notices that Din-Din has located his mother. That's all that he needed to see to know that it was time to stop pretending to be helpless.

As Cho -Goon approaches the back of the first wagon he unlatches it and several rocks fall to the ground. While he was unlatching, Brianna had run over to several Wachooti that were shackled, and grabbed one by the hand. At least six of them were all shackled together, so she ended up pulling all of them towards the wagon.

She then reached down and started handing large rocks to each of the Wachooti prisoners, after the last rock was handed out, she screamed: "Rock fiiiiiiiiight!"

She then launched a rock and hit the nearest soldier in the head with a rock and it stunned the soldier causing it to cover its head and move away. She looked over at the Wachooti prisoners and motioned for them to throw their rocks and they began throwing their rocks at the other soldiers. All of the prisoners saw that throwing the rocks proved to be effective and almost instantly a race of peaceful beings began throwing rocks like angry savages and pelting their captors causing them to retreat.

They all began using the rocks to break the electrical cords that bond them together.

Austin began rising up while being held down. He let out a growl, turned scream, during the movement. The big reptilian being jumps back and pulls a club type of weapon from his belt. Austin snatched both soldiers holding him towards each other causing them to bump heads and fall down. The big soldier moves towards Austin and swings the club with his right hand and Austin immediately catches it with his left hand, grabs the soldier's neck with the right and hip tosses him into a hard slam to the ground.

Cho-Goon pushes towards Din-Din and hits one of the soldiers with a rock on the side of its head while it wasn't looking. The other soldier releases Din-Din and engages Cho-Goon, but Din-Din dives for the legs of the soldier and Cho-Goon takes the top, they succeed at tackling the soldier to the ground. At this point all of the Wachooti people have been freed and are now throwing rocks at the soldiers causing some to retreat and the rest to take cover appearing to look helpless, almost as if they have never experienced anything like this, almost as if they've never had to think and fight on their own. For the first time they have no one to give commands, no one to think for them. Where is their leader?

Brianna finds her way to Austin and as he looks for soldiers to fight.

Brianna: "Boy when we get back home, you're gonna have to explain how your sister had to save you from an army of lizard dudes!"

Austin: "It was my plan!"

Brianna: "Yeah, but I executed the plan and saved you!"

Austin: "You know what, you're right, you saved me, ole "Gunshow Gonzales" saved us all!" (Both of the teens laugh then Austin stops abruptly when he sees lord Kull running toward the biggest ship out of the three in the distance.)

Austin: "No way!"

Brianna: "No way what?"

Austin: "He made it here from Earth! It's time to finish him once and for all!"

Brianna: "You mean the one who escaped?" (with fear in her eyes)

Austin: "Yeah, go and make sure Din-Din and his family are safe!"

Brianna: "I'm not going anywhere, we will defeat him together, gun show style!" (While flexing) (Austin turns around and looks at Brianna)

Austin: "Ummmm yeah, that felt weird, kinda cheesy."

Brianna: "I'll work on it."

Austin: "Good, let's go."

The Wachooti people never practiced nor believed in war or violence, but proved to be overpowering their enemy once they decided to defend their home. A group of them assembled and began tying up the soldiers and putting them into the wagon like cages. The fight was now in full swing and all that Din-Din could think about was getting his family to safety.

Cho-Goon is seen approaching Din-Din as he hugs his mother.

Cho-Goon: "Where are the little ones?"

Din-Din: "They are with Ms. Pincey."

Din-Din's father: "Dineckdin!"

Din-Din: "Father!"

The family run towards each other and all hug with tears in their eyes and smiles on their faces.

Din-Din: "Stay close, I refuse to let anything happen to my family again. I must finish the job of repairing the harmonic defense system, follow me."

Din-Din, his family and new ally Cho-Goon all take off into the direction towards the lab which is on the edge of town to gather tools. On their way they spotted many of the lizard soldiers retreating into the forest areas for a place to hide from the Wachooti.

Brianna: "How do you know which ship he ran to?"

Austin: "Use your magic and tell me which one he went to."

Brianna: "She doesn't work that way." (Austin stops walking)

Austin: "She?"

Brianna: "Yeah, she's me, it's a long story I'll tell you later."

Austin: "So you hear voices in your head now, I really gotta get us back home, we're hearing voices in our heads an..."

Brianna: "Wait you're hearing voices in your head too!? What the hell is going on!?"

Austin: "Yeah it was a creepy guy with a hood on and he said he wanted to add me to his collection and he was touching my arms and legs."

Brianna: "Whoa! You got molested by a creepy space pimp and you didn't tell me, I mean I know that was hard to tell someone but daaaaang. What else did he do? Lemme guess you don't wanna talk about it?"

Austin: "Hey! Easy! That was it, then I woke up on the spaceship on the way here."

Brianna: "Oh snap, that's when you punched ole boy and almost killed em, wow!"

Austin: "We can try to figure all that out later, look at the ships and find this giant lizard because he's the reason behind all of this madness."

Brianna: "Ok, hold on. (looking left and right) Ok, ok, I can see his energy, well I think it's his energy."

Austin: "What does it read?"

Brianna: "It's back and forth between 89 and 97"

Austin: "That's got to be him, which ship?"

Brianna: "The middle one, the biggest one, about 100 yards in the rear entrance."

Austin: "Ok, let's hurry!"

The two teens dart off towards the rear entrance of the giant ship. From a distance the legs of the ship that held it up seemed small but up close were the size of school buses standing straight up. As they got to the ramp of the ship it had a constant hum as if it was on but running idle.

Brianna: "It feels like we're entering a huge building!"

Austin: "Yeah, it feels very strange like it has its own atmosphere."

Brianna: "It just feels like we shouldn't be in here."

A noise up ahead made them stop moving and wait to see what made the noise. As they stood still, two lizard-like beings in white plastic suits appear in front of them walking with what looks to be a table that was hovering off the ground and moving with them.

The lizard-like beings let out a few click sounds and continued down the ramp right past Austin and Brianna as if they weren't a threat.

Austin: "Ok, let's keep going."

Brianna: "It's about 56 yards ahead, this doesn't even seem like we're inside of a spaceship, it's like a big cruise ship."

Austin: "Shhhh! Do you hear that?"

Din-Din and the rest of the group has just made it to his workshop on the edge of the trail outside of the little city.

Din-Din: "I have everything ready to go give me a second."

Cho-Goon: "I will stand watch."

The sound of people yelling and rustling through leaves and bushes were everywhere. Even though it seemed as if the Wachooti had fought and taken back their home, there still was a level of uncertainty.

Din-Din: "Ok, let's go, follow me!"

They all take off towards the harmonic defense system at the top of the hill overlooking the city.

Lord Kull: "Where is it! (he screams at one of the chief scientists) Where is the elixir?!"

Chief scientist: "My lord it is not yet ready, it's just not stable enough for consumption."(as he stands guarding three vials filled with red liquid and a double helix inside of them)

Lord Kull growled as he pushed the chief scientist across the floor knocking over trays and shattering several glass jars. Two scientists take off out of the corridor and soon the third that was pushed down, followed.

The teens only heard roars and clicks as they shuffled quietly from corridor to corridor looking for the source until they saw the lizard people with lab coats running from the room up on the right.

Brianna: "Whoa, I heard that one!" (After hearing the growl and the glass breaking) "Over there!"

The two run past the scientists running away and enter the room just in time to see Lord Kull facing them with three red vials in his hand. (Touching his translation device on his neck)

Lord Kull: "You shouldn't have come here. You are meddling with a force that will never be stopped! This ship, this planet, this universe belongs to us! You are a mere measly carrgon waiting to be smashed under the boot of the order!"

Austin looked to his left at Brianna and says: "I wonder if everyone from his planet is this long winded?"

Brianna: "I was thinking the same thing, I thought he was never going to stop!"

(Both teens laugh hysterically for a moment)

Brianna: "Wait, didn't you already kick his ass?!"

Austin: "Yeah, then he got up and ran, to another planet."

(They both laugh hysterically again until Lord Kull yells)

Lord Kull: "We shall see who laughs last as you witness my power!"

(He unscrews one of the vials and swallows the contents whole as he looks at the ceiling)

In seconds the giant starts to moan as if he was in pain. He clutched his stomach and doubled over and the teens noticed that the back of his suit ripped down the middle.

Brianna: "Did you see that?"

The boots that he had on split open and his hands almost doubled in size as he let out a long deep howl. They could hear his bones crunching as his body grew bigger right in front of them.

Austin: "Run!" (The teens bolt out in the same fashion as the scientists)

Lord Kull: "Aaaaaaaa whooooos running nooooow!!"

As he stands up and begins to walk awkwardly due to one leg being bigger than the other and other mutations taking place. (He was becoming a gigantic monstrosity and fast.)

Austin: "We have to make it off of this ship, we need space and weapons!"

Brianna: "The only weapons here are rocks!"

Austin: "Rocks! You gotta be kidding me! Well, I need a big rock to put this dude away!"

203

Lord Kull is seen running after them, but much slower and sort of like a leap, one leg at a time. He is starting to look less mutated, but he has tripled in size and muscle mass as his body was adjusting to the changes. The elixir that Lord Kull ingested is a science experiment created by Master On'Doon, as a gift to Lord Kull. It was a wish of Lord Kull to boost his strength, that was granted by Master On'Doon. He named it the Nova gene, and once ingested, all of your physical attribute's skyrocket, but only for a fraction of time.

The chief scientist who tried to warn Lord Kull was in charge of testing the elixir on cloned subjects. The subjects had to be terminated due to becoming enraged and uncontrollable.

The teens make it to the large landing ramp and begin to descend towards the ground. Just as they were on their way down there was a huge fight at the bottom of the ramp between a group of Wachooti and the entire science group that tried to evacuate the ship.

Brianna: "We are headed right into a fight!"

Austin: "How strong are they?"

Brianna: "Nobody over a level nine!"

Austin: "Well, good luck to them because the fight is coming to the...."

As he says that a loud roar comes from the top of the landing ramp and all of the fighting stops. Everyone looks to the top of the ramp to see the new and improved Lord Kull.

As Brianna and Austin speed past them to find a safe place.

Lord Kull jumps and lands halfway down the landing ramp, grabs one of the onlooking scientists and throws him at Austin, hitting him in the back, knocking him down into the dirt onto his chest. Brianna runs over and grabs him by the hand to help him up.

Brianna: "Hurry up, he's coming for us!"

The angry, pain filled roars coming from Lord Kull let you know that he was still somewhat in some kind of transition. The ones that stood at the end of the ramp polarized by the sight of him got knocked down and pretty much ran over. The only thing on Lord Kull's mind was destroying Austin and he had tunnel vision.

Austin: "We can't run from him, I have to stay and fight, go find a safe place to hide!"

Brianna: "I didn't want to tell you this but, his power level has jumped to over three hundred and I'm scared for you!"

Austin snaps out of his hurt and looks at Brianna and says: "So you don't believe that I can beat him?" (With fear in his eyes)

Brianna: "It's not just about you losing to him, but if he does beat you, we will be slaves, to him and whatever other creatures! We will never see Earth again! I don't wanna die!"

(As she bursts into tears)

As she cries Austin sheds a tear and stands up. Her eyes have a frightened look as he reaches for her.

Brianna: "Look out!"

Austin turns around just in time to see Lord Kull has thrown a large tree branch. He is knocked back by the tree branch but he caught it!

Austin: "Thanks!"

(While positioning the tree branch so that he can swing it like baseball bat)

Austin: "Brianna, get out of here!"

Austin begins to walk towards Lord Kull dragging the large tree branch with one hand with an angry look on his face.

Austin: "I beat you fair and square on Earth and you just couldn't let it go, you even took performance enhancing drugs! I'm going to end you this time!"

Lord Kull: "You are nothing!" (In a gurgling voice as if he was choking on fluid)

 Austin: (chanting to himself) "I am faster, smarter and stronger than evil." (he says this repeatedly while walking up)

Din-Din reached the end of the trail and stood at the base of the Harmonic Defense System.

Din-Din: "I don't know how I'm going to do this or how long it's going to take, but I know that this is the key to saving our planet, and it is the final step! I can feel it!"

Cho-Goon: "Whatever you need from me, I am at your disposal."

Din-Din: "Grab the tools and come with me to the rear of the machine, everyone else look after the little ones and pray to the ancestors that we are victorious in our efforts!"

As Cho-Goon and Din-Din begin looking for the main components of the machine, the war below wages on. Austin and Lord Kull circle each other until Lord Kull reaches to grab Austin. Austin ducks the grab and swings the tree, hitting Lord Kull in the shins. Part of the tree branch broke off on impact but Austin still had a big piece in his hands.

Lord Kull had grown so big that his every move was slower, making it easy for Austin to move away from him. On Lord Kull's second attempt to grab Austin, he missed again, leaving his back exposed and Austin swung what was left of the tree branch as hard as he could breaking it on Lord Kull's lower back causing him to let out a roar.

Even though he was bigger and stronger he still felt pain and that's all that Austin needed to know. Kull turns around and lunges toward Austin, as Austin goes to move, he trips and stumbles to the ground. Lord Kull grabs Austin by the back with his left hand and raises him up high and looks him in the face and lets out a loud shriek.

Lord Kull: "I'm going to destroy you!" (As he begins punching Austin in the stomach with his right hand) The punches were so hard that Austin started out bracing for them and by the third punch he was slowly starting to fade.

Lord Kull: "Just as I said, you are nothing! (dropping Austin to the ground at his feet) Just a bag of meat!" (as he takes a step up and kicks Austin in the stomach and sends him flying into the side of a wagon filled with rocks)

The wagon collapsed and all of the rocks began rolling out on top of Austin.

Brianna walks into the view.

Brianna: "Where can I hit this monster to cause the most pain?"

Voice: "Optic, genitalia, any lower digits?"

Brianna: "What?!"

Voice: "Eyes, penis or feet."

Brianna: "Say it like that next time!"

Voice: "As you wish."

Brianna: "Ayyyy! Over here ugly!" (as she tosses a rock up and down in her right hand)

In the distance there was a group of Wachooti beating some soldiers to the ground with rocks until they took notice of the monstrously large being moving towards the area where they were fighting. A few took off running while the others were seen watching him come closer.

Lord Kull: "I will chew your bones!" (While picking up speed towards Brianna)

Brianna moves in front of one of the several large wagons, and waits until Kull is close enough, and launches a medium sized rock towards his genital area. Kull is hit with the rock that basically bounces off of him like a flea. He then lunges for her as she ducks underneath the wagon and hurries out on the other side. He follows her underneath the wagon and gets stuck; his head and hands are the only things visible on the other side of the wagon, so she grabs a larger boulder like rock and slams it onto the top of Kull's head and takes off into the nearby wooded area. The boulder destroys his translator upon impact, leaving him screaming like a dinosaur. Austin is starting to wake up and recover from the punishment that he took to realize that he was practically buried under wood and rocks.

Cho-Goon: "Does this device operate using sound?"

Din-Din: "I believe it does but I don't know how it…"

Cho-Goon: "I see!" (as he steps back to examine the large statue like device)

He starts to rub around the base of the statue as Din-Din watches, eagerly waiting to see what Cho-Goon has discovered.

Cho-Goon: "Ah ha!" (His fingers slide across a small sliding door that was concealed at the far bottom of the statue, he slides it open.)

Inside of the large device was a machine wedged between two large pieces, of what looked like Wachootium, but the Wachootium looked to be burned or damaged.

Din-Din: "Bless the ancient ones! You have shined the light!" (as he grabs his tools and gets closer to examine the machine.)

Cho-Goon: "It looks like it makes sound, like a music machine"

Din-Din: "What is a music machine?"

Cho-Goon: "Hmmmmm, but how is it powered?"

Din-Din: "Well that's easy, I've been using Wachootium to po…(his eyes light up as he stands up) That's it my friend we've solved it! We've solved the great mystery!"

Cho-Goon: "But we've done nothing!" (looking confused)

Din-Din reaches into the device and begins trying to remove the damaged Wachootium and learn how it all connects.

Lord Kull roars while trapped under the wagon, as Brianna watches from some nearby bushes. He then lifts the wagon on his back in a push up position and stands up dumping the entire wagon of rocks and breaking the wagon to pieces. Brianna screams and Austin hears her, plus the noise from the wagon, and begins to unbury himself in a hurry.

Lord Kull: "No one will be able to save you once I get my hands on you! I can smell your fear; it's oozing from your skin!" (He thought that he was speaking in a language that she could understand but all she heard was a series of growls and roars)

He storms over to the bushes and starts moving them around looking for Brianna. She covers her mouth as he gets closer to her hiding spot. He spots her sneaker and grabs her by her foot and picks her up by the ankle. Austin runs up to see his sister being dangled by her ankle in the air. He picks up a large boulder and launches it at Lord Kull's back and takes off running behind the rock. As the rock hits Lord Kull in the back, he drops Brianna and turns around to a punishing punch to the face from Austin knocking him down. Brianna gets up and runs behind Austin and then runs to find a hiding place.

Austin: "Let's finish this!"

Lord Kull gets up and grabs a piece of the broken wagon and swings it at Austin while roaring loudly. Austin ducks the swing and rushes towards Kull to deliver another punch. Lord Kull swings again knocking Austin to the ground and rushes over with the broken piece of the wagon and attempts to choke Austin with it. Austin grabs it with both hands to try to stop him. The two struggle back and forth on the ground.

Din-Din: "Wait here I will be right back!"

Cho-Goon: "But where are you going?"

Din-Din: "To grab some Wachootium, we need Wachootium to power the device!" (as he runs off down the trail full speed)

Cho-Goon hurries back to try to understand what Din-Din just told him.

With the force of Lord Kull pushing a large piece of wood onto his neck Austin is seen struggling to push back.

Lord Kull: "You are no match for my power, submit to the great Lord Kull!"

With all of his might Austin began pushing so hard that you could see the tears starting to fall from the corners of his eyes. Lord Kull begins to panic as Austin proceeds to lift the stick off of his neck, so he punches Austin in the side quickly to regain control of the exchange.

Brianna screams in the background.

Brianna: "We all need you to get up! Get up and win this fight or we will all be killed. What did we come here to do?!"

Din-Din had always kept a few large chunks of Wachootium in his little lab because he was always trying to make new things with it. So, he was headed there in full speed.

"This is it!" he thought.

He was already a hero but this will definitely solidify his place in society as a scientist and a scholar. He busted through the door of the lab and went rummaging through all of his storage and found several large brick-like pieces and shoved them into a cloth bag and sprang back out the door.

Austin was certain that Lord Kull was going to kill him, but he couldn't give up. The large log like stick was against his face. He knew that this was his last shot to get Kull off of him.

Din-Din arrived back to the hds and found Cho-Goon cleaning out the area where the damaged Wachootium was positioned. He pulls out two large pieces and began trying to figure out how to place the first piece. Then without any effort the first piece snapped right into place as if it was magnetized and it startled Din-Din. He smiled and grabbed the other piece and it snapped into place, the two stood there waiting to see what would happen.

Austin began his final push to get the monster off of him. He had a brief flashback of all that he has been through since learning to believe in himself and realized that he was victorious every time that he faced an enemy or a challenge.

Brianna: "Get up! Get up right now, the only reason that you've kept us alive is because you believed in yourself!

214

That's what Din-Din has been trying to tell you the whole time! We believe that you are a hero!"

Austin goes from a low grunt to a loud scream and begins to lift Lord Kull off of him. Lord Kull tries his hardest to push back but it wasn't working this time.

As Din-Din and Cho-Goon stare at the machine, they hear a clicking sound and they move closer to see what the noise was. Attached to a box was a little "L" shaped handle with a square piece on the end, like it's used to wind something up. The handle started to move up to one piece of Wachootium, then down to the other, in a winding motion. Slowly at first and then it started to pick up speed until you could hardly see the handle anymore it was moving so fast.

Then everything started to vibrate. At first it felt like a tickle going up the spine, whatever that was happening must've been very pleasant because everyone had a big smile on their faces. The vibrations got faster and faster until they could no longer feel it, as if everything was normal.

Austin and everyone in the area felt it as well, but Lord Kull was feeling something different.

He started to make strange noises and his body appeared to be coming down in size. In front of everyone he was coming undone, the nova gene was wearing off. Austin began walking up and threw the stick down and held his right fist inside of his left hand as he stared at Lord Kull.

Brianna: "He's getting weaker, get him!!!"

Austin springs forward and delivers a powerful right hook that took Lord Kull off of his feet backwards, but Austin caught him by the ankle and swung him into the opposite direction directly into a huge pile of rocks. Lord Kull hit the rocks hard and hopped up quickly as he was met with a punch that caused a flash of light that sat him back down on top of the rocks dazed. The flash of light was seen by everyone on the top of the cliff where the harmonic defense system sits

Din-Din: "Austin!" (he immediately started running to the trail back down into the town beneath the cliff and Cho-Goon followed)

Austin: "That felt really good, get up!"

Lord Kull gets up. (he's pretty much back to his regular size which was pretty big to begin with but his body language was showing defeat)

Lord Kull: "Finish the job!" (As he motions for Austin to come closer)

As Austin takes the invite to swing, Lord Kull catches his arm and hip tosses him to the ground and stood up with a loud roar. Austin thought that the fight was over but the slam proved that he had a good amount of power left because it knocked the wind out of him. He sat up and was hit in the chest by both of Lord Kull's fists, hammering him to the ground again. Austin's entire midsection felt as if every bone was broken. Lord Kull turns to the crowd of Wachooti and some soldiers that were watching.

Lord Kull: "I am your ruler! This is what happens when you disobey my commands!"

The crowd pays no attention to him as they start whispering to one another as they see Austin get up holding his stomach with blood coming from his mouth.

Austin: "It's over, you will never rule this planet or any other planet, evil never wins!"

Lord Kull turns around and charges Austin and everything slowed down as Austin screamed: "Kaboom!" at the top of his lungs while swinging a punch and thinking of a bomb exploding at the tip of his fist.

Brianna: "Oh sh...!'" (As her energy reader starts to climb higher and higher)

As his fist connected with Lord Kull's jaw, a huge orb of white light appeared, followed by an explosion that sent Austin and Lord Kull flying backwards away from each other. An almost thirty-foot-wide crater was created on the ground where the punch landed. Brianna's eye attachment went all the way up to 1000 and stopped working right before the punch landed. Everyone close enough to see the punch was knocked down and dazed from the powerful explosion. They are all seen sitting up and looking around at each other. A huge dust cloud surrounding everyone with a loud ringing sound in everyone's ears is all that was left of the fight.

Din-Din and Cho-Goon are seen running up to the area.

Din-Din: "What happened? Where's Austin!?"

Brianna: "We have to find him!" They went into the direction that they Thought he might be in.

Brianna: "This is where he was before the explosion, so he has to be over here somewhere!"

As they all scramble to find Austin, he is seen walking up dusting himself off.

Brianna: "What happened?!"

Austin: "Where is he, I need to make sure that he is finished this time!"

Everyone turns around and starts to look for Lord Kull.

Brianna: "Maybe he exploded into dust! Over there!"

Lord Kull was headed away from the city area at a high rate of speed

Brianna: "He's moving incredibly fast!" (while watching his speed accelerate)

Austin starts running as fast as he could in the direction of Lord Kull and Brianna follows. Lord Kull had a healthy head start so he had already travelled a good distance ahead of Austin.

Brianna: "He just stopped!"

At that very moment they all heard the sound of a ship initiating a launch.

Austin: "Nooooo!" (As he looks around on the ground frantically)

Austin spots a nice sized rock and reaches for it with both hands. As the ship begins to lift off of the ground, Austin begins running towards it with the big rock. The ship starts to move quickly in an arc attempting to leave and Austin throws the rock with all of his might at the ship. The ship is a cruiser only meant for exploration and emergency evacuation but it was the only thing that Lord Kull had to escape.

Brianna: "I think you missed, good try though!"

Austin: "Hold on..."

The ship started to follow an arc pattern while the rock was moving in a straight line, but the arc was headed into the path of the rock.

Brianna: "Wait! How...?"

Austin: "Shhhhhhh! Come on, come on..."

All of a sudden, the rock hit the ship.

Austin: "Booooom!!"

It sounded like a car crash and everyone made noises of excitement when the rock struck the ship. The ship swerved and debris fell out of the sky while a heavy black smoke came from the ship. It accelerated faster and soon disappeared into the clouds. Austin dropped to the ground on his knees as he watched the ship disappear. Din-Din walked up behind Austin and put his hand on his shoulder.

Din-Din: "Don't worry, we won't be seeing him again."

Austin: "I failed, he's just going to do the same thing to another planet."

Din-Din: "Stand up! You are a hero! You have saved my family and my planet! You have also saved your family and your planet. Be proud of yourself, we are all alive because of you!"

Brianna: "He's right Austin, you've done something that nobody can ever say that they did! That's special! Sit with that for a moment! You saved planets!" (with a huge smile on her face)

Austin stood up and started dusting himself off.

Austin: "You guys are right; I think it will take a while to process everything that happened here and on Earth. Speaking of Earth, I know that our moms are freaking out about us leaving on a spaceship."

Din-Din: "Yes! We will prepare the ship shortly to get you back home!"

Cho-Goon: "I will prepare the ship immediately master!"

Brianna: "Wait, where is Cho-Goon going to go?"

Din-Din: "He is welcomed to make our planet his new home."

Cho-Goon turns around and can't believe that for the first time since he can remember in his life, he can say that he's free to do whatever he wants.

Cho-Goon: "My new friend, I would greatly appreciate that!"

Din-Din: "Then it's done! Come let me show you around before you leave, I have a feeling that this won't be the last time you visit."

As they all begin to walk away, you can see Wachooti people and the lizard soldiers helping each other and beginning to clean up everywhere.

Austin and Brianna got a chance to meet the elders and were both given permission to come back whenever they wanted to. They also participated in a small ceremony where they tried "tuck tuck" a cultural fish dish that the Wachooti people loved to eat during special occasions.

Austin: "We have never been to any planet other than Earth, so this was a very special experience for us, thank you to all of you for treating us like family. We have family on Earth and I know that they are worried about us so we must begin our journey back home."

Cho-Goon: "Master, Dineckdin and I, have agreed to travel together to get you back to Earth."

Austin: "Ok, let's get going."

Cho-Goon: "I have re-fueled the ship and set our navigation system for Earth."

Austin, Brianna, Din-Din and Cho-Goon take the walk on the trail towards the ship.

Quintan Bizzell

The Order of The Nine

Brianna: "It seems a lot longer going back to the ship. Cho-Goon why didn't you bring the ship closer!?"

Cho-Goon: "I found it rather peaceful to take the walk and enjoy this nice planet that I can now call home." (with a smile on his face)

The ship was coming into view as the four continued their walk.

Din-Din: "By the next time we meet, I will have a new set of bracers with even more power for your next adventure."

Austin: "Next adventure? Who said that I will have a next adventure?"

Din-Din: "Being a hero is your job now, and now that everyone knows what you did, you will be very busy" (with a smile on his face)

Brianna: "Well, you are a hero now so it does kinda make sense. I actually saved a hero though, so what does that make me?"

Everyone chuckles

Austin: "It makes you a dope little sister! Alright let's get back to Earth!"

They all enter the ship one by one and the ramp slowly lifts and closes. With a few button clicks, the ship begins to move upward into the sky slowly.

Austin and Brianna look out of the window at the landscape as it slowly starts to fade.

Brianna: "We have to come back because we didn't even get to explore the planet, it looks so cool!"

Din-Din: "It is actually quite warm and humid most days with a nice breeze when the sun leaves."

Austin: "She meant cool, as in awesome."

Din-Din: "What is awesome?"

Austin: "I see where this is goi..."

His right ear began to ring so loud that he couldn't even hear the ship or anything anymore and apparently everyone else was experiencing the same thing because they all looked around at each other. The ringing stopped and a holographic image appeared smack dab in the middle of everyone on the ship.

Brianna: "Are we all...?"

"Yes!"

Everyone chimed in at the same time. The image in the hologram was of a figure that appeared to be very tall with almost silver hair but it was a hologram. The figure had on all white with an all-white hood covering its face. Instantly it felt as if all the air was sucked out of the vessel. Austin looked around and they were no longer inside of the ship.

Brianna: "Just when I thought things were going back to normal."

Austin: "I have a feeling that nothing will ever be normal again."

Voice: "Hello, and welcome."

Austin: "Hi, where are we? And what is your name?"

Voice: "I have many names, and we will get into that later. Right now, we want to welcome you to our celebration."

Austin: "Thanks for welcoming us but when you said "we" it kinda threw me off because I only see you."

Voice: "Oh, please excuse my forgetfulness."

As he snaps his fingers softly the room begins to fill with objects and creatures walking around as if it was a party. There was music playing and things flying around overhead like little metal balls that were scanning people. The weird part was that Austin and his crew were seated at a huge table facing eight other beings that were all different biologically and they were watching Austin's every move.

They did not speak they only watched.

Austin: "Wow! That was amazing! Where are we again!?"

Voice: "You are somewhere that doesn't exist; therefore, it has no name, hard to explain, but I've created this space for our celebration."

Austin: "Nice! What are we celebrating!?"

Voice: "You."

As everyone in the party stops what they were doing and turns to look at Austin. Austin looks around at all of the different faces and they all look to be from other worlds, he and Brianna were the only humans there.

Austin: "What did I do to deserve a celebration?"

Voice: "It's not what you did, it's what we've watched you become."

Austin: "You've all been watching me, but how?"

Voice: "We've had our eye on you since birth. We've seen all of the trials that you and your family endured and we are proud to see that through it all you still chose to be a hero and protector of those that need help. We would like to extend our hands and offer you a seat to complete our council. We have nine seats, but only eight members, should you choose to join us, you will complete the "Order of the Nine"."

Austin: "This is a lot to take in…"

Voice: "It is a big job being the champion and protector of Earth. Take some time and enjoy your celebration while you think about your decision. Music please." (as he softly snaps his fingers the music begins to play and everyone goes back to talking and eating)

A small metal orb flies up to Brianna and scans her with a green laser up and down.

Brianna: "I wonder what that was about?"

The orb lowers itself to the table and a plate with chicken fingers, fries and a bottle of soda materializes in front of her.

Brianna: "Wait! How did it know that I wanted that?! That was the first thing on my mind to get when we got back to Earth! Where do I get one of these!? This must be heaven!" (As she starts to eat and look around at everything.)

Din-Din shuffles over to Austin, who appears to still be in disbelief. "You've made it! You are very special if they've been watching you since birth. What a great opportunity you have! I knew it when I saw you!"

Cho Goon approaches and smiles at Austin as well.

Cho Goon: "Well Master you have been offered the highest honor and opportunity that exists, whatever you choose I will be by your side." (as he pats Austin on his shoulder)

Austin: "Thanks guys!"

The metal orb positioned itself right in front of Austin and began scanning him with a green laser like light. Everything in his body was telling him to accept the invitation, but the fear of the powerful things he may have to face like Lord Kull has him questioning if that's what he wants to do. While he was thinking, a plate of hot steamy, buttery French toast with syrup and a glass of milk with two ice cubes just the way his mom makes it appeared in front of him.

Austin: "Oh my god! Yes!"

The party stopped.

Someone says: "He said yes, hooray!"

(The party went crazy with joy and everyone continued to talk and dance)

Austin: "Hey wait!" (with a mouth full of French toast)

Brianna: "Did you say yes?" (With a huge smile on her face)

Austin: "I did but..."

Brianna: "This will be dope! I can't wait for the next adventure!"

Austin gets approached by the tall one with the white hair and all white cloak.

Tall man: "Is it true that you have made a choice?"

Austin: "I was scared at first, but seeing everyone's reactions to me saying yes, I proudly accept the responsibility and claim my seat as the ninth member of the Order of the Nine!"

Tall man: "Everyone! May I have your attention! We now have a protector and representative for the third planet, Earth! We have waited for so long and now everything has aligned!"

The crowd begins to clap and chat with one another about the news. The tall man begins to snap his fingers softly and everyone in the party begins to disappear little by little.

Austin: "Why is everyone leaving?"

Tall man: "They were only here to witness the naming of Earth's protector, now it is time for a little history and information. First things first, the eight other members sitting here at this table are representatives of eight out of the nine planets in this solar system."

Brianna: "But, isn't Pluto a dwarf planet and not considered to be a planet?"

Tall man: "Pluto may be what Earth calls a dwarf planet, but a planet nonetheless. Just because Earth people name things doesn't make it law little one." (As he smiles and winks)

"Moving forward, the eight other members are tasked with defending their assigned planet and protecting the lives of the species on their planets. We call on each other for help to protect our solar system, we join together and stop the threat. Yes, we have been monitoring you since birth. You and many others are a part of what we call "the star seed program" on Earth. You are very special to our universe. The program started long ago with a mission to raise the vibration of Earth and help us create peace."

Din-Din: "I knew it, you were born to be a hero." (with a smile on his face)

Austin: "I noticed that everyone else here has a seat at the table, what about you?"

Tall man: "I am what most would call a builder, my bloodline is ancient. Our job is to seed planets with life and look after every planet that has been seeded. It was and still is an ongoing process that started a very long time ago. You will learn more about everything in time young star seed. Oridio On'Doon was also a part of the ancient builder race. He was different from the beginning; he was always obsessed with creating one single species that would conquer all other species. He no longer cared for seeding planets and looking after the inhabitants instead he began playing God, creating his own species of life for his personal collection. He started seeking out planets that already have inhabitants, enslaving the inhabitants, then destroying the planets. The complete opposite of our life purpose given to us by the creator. He has created an army and seeks to destroy everything that we have built. No one knows what his plan is at this time but we have to assume that he wants to destroy life on every planet he touches. Austin, your bravery has just sparked the resistance that we needed to fight back and protect life on all planets. No one has ever stepped up to do what you just did. You are a hero to us all!"

Austin: "Wow! I don't know what to say."

Tall man: "Now that you have accepted the job, we will be in contact."

Tall man starts to softly snap his fingers and things start to disappear one by one until everything in their surroundings turns back into the ship that they were on. A series of noises from the ship snaps everyone out of their daze.

Brianna: "That was probably the coolest thing that I have ever experienced in my life!"

Austin: "And it was all in our heads, we were in the ship the whole time!"

Brianna: "If it was all in our heads then explain why I'm still full from the food, and you have syrup on your shirt!?"

Austin looks down at his shirt in wonder.

Cho-Goon: "I have heard stories of the tall one in all white, now I realize that all the stories were true…"

Din-Din: "The coordinates have been set and we are ready."

Austin: "Ok…"

Brianna interrupts.

Brianna: "Make it so!"

Everyone laughs and the ship goes into warp headed to Earth.

Din-Din had a huge smile while navigating the ship as if he was daydreaming about something pleasant.

Austin: "It's good to see you smile again!"

Din-Din: "This is the happiest time of my life, I dreamed of this and it is now coming true! The elders have asked me to teach about technology and Cho-Goon will be my partner. I will have my own home and a seat with the elders as an advisor!"

Cho-Goon: "I didn't know that I would be assisting you." (with a smile)

Din-Din: "I know, it was a surprise, but I couldn't wait!"

Austin: "Wow! That's great Din-Din!"

As Brianna comes over and gives him a huge hug.

Din-Din: "I am no longer looked down on and made fun of. I am now held high, like a hero!" Cho-Goon: "We are coming out of warp and entering the Earth's atmosphere. Brace yourselves." Din-Din: "Initiating the cloaking device."

Brianna: "Wow! Everybody sounds so professional, like the X-men!" (as she chuckles)

Cho-Goon: "This is it."

The ship begins to descend down from the clouds. The view begins to get clear of the apartment buildings and the surrounding neighborhood, as well as all of the damage from the battle that took place.

Austin: "See, I told you we would make it back home." (With a smile on his face)

Din-Din: "Starting the landing sequence."

As the ship lowers down to land, you can see graffiti that says: "Come back for us!" in big bold letters on the ground of the rooftop. Just as the landing ramp comes down, Brianna runs down the ramp and what appears to be a homeless person who was sleeping in the corner jumps up and says: "They've come back!!!" repeatedly, as he runs down the apartment stairs that led to the roof.

Austin walks down the ramp and notices that Din-Din and Cho-Goon are not following behind. Austin: "You guys coming or what?"

Din-Din: "We must return quickly; we have many big plans to begin working on."

Austin: "Yeah, but I thought you guys would hangout for a while before you left, but I understand you're a hero now."

Din-Din: "And so are you!" (As you hear Austin's name being chanted by a big crowd in the parking lot below)

Brianna eyes get big while hugging Din-Din as she hears the people. She runs over to take a look and sees that the parking lot is full.

Brianna: "Oh my god Austin, this is crazy!"

Cho-Goon: "Looks like you will be busy as well Master!" (With a smile)

Din-Din: "We are not far away, when it's time we'll be ready!"

Cho-Goon: "I am forever in debt to you, you freed me!" (As they shook hands)

They begin to go back up the ramp to the ship and the ramp retracted and the ship lifted. The emergency door for the apartment stairs flew open, Bonnie Jones and Chandra Gonzales burst through with happy tears.

Brianna: "Mom!"

Austin ran to his mother and hugged her tight. In the parking lot below, while the crowd was chanting and cheering, Jimmy appears. He was looking around on the ground. He didn't seem to be interested in chanting and cheering for Austin. He looked like he was on a mission. He removed some rubble from a few areas and his eyes grew large with happiness.

Jimmy: "I knew it was true! Finally!" (As he lifted Cho-Goon's whip and stared at it while he began to run away from the area laughing)

The End